# GUARDIAN ANGEL

Kayla Klanreungsang

PUBLISHED BY

SIGMA'S
BOOKSHELF

MINNETONKA, MN 55305
WWW.SIGMASBOOKSHELF.COM

Guardian Angel by Kayla Klanreungsang

Printed in the United States of America

Author photo by Jennifer's Short and Sweet Photography.

First Printing 2017

ISBN 978-0-9987157-5-9

guard•i•an an•gel
/ˈgärdēən ˈ,ānjəl/
noun
a spirit that is believed to watch over
and protect a person or place.

# Chapter One

I walked outside. The chilly autumn wind nipped and bit at any of my exposed skin that had managed to peek out from under my layers of warm clothing. One thing was for sure. I had never experienced an autumn as cold as this one.

It was only mid-October and already the sky was gray and gloomy, threatening the town of Brookhaven with snow. I wrapped my coat tighter around myself and pulled my hat down to cover my ears. I scowled at the numbness in my hands.

It wasn't that I hated the winter months, but that I strongly disliked how long it took to get ready. Not to mention the fact that almost every day I forgot something. Today, it had been my mittens. Shoving my hands into my pockets, I continued my lengthy trek to school, at least it felt long. Rationally, I knew that a twenty-minute walk wasn't actually that long, but it sure felt like it, and the weather made sure of it.

Okay, maybe I lied. I did hate the cold. Every winter for as long as I could remember, I had despised it and everything that came along with it. I didn't see how anyone could enjoy themselves with the constant clattering of teeth and violent shivering. It made no logical sense. My toes felt frozen.

They were even starting to go numb, and I knew it was a sign that I needed new boots. I simply could not reuse the ones from last year. I sighed because I had quite liked that pair, and knew it would be difficult for me to find another comfortable pair that fit properly.

When I looked up from my poor shoes, I saw my school, big and dark. The building seemed to tower over everything, and it was not a place I enjoyed spending a good part of my teenage years at. I couldn't wait to escape this school and this town. I had lived in Brookhaven for as long as I could remember, but the only thoughts that were ever on my mind these days proved that I had no connection to the place. Get out. It was all I had ever wanted and I was so close. Two more years, I thought. Two more years and I could leave. And believe me when I said I couldn't wait.

I was just starting my junior year in high school, which left me with two excruciating years before I could pack up and leave. No one would miss me. Both my parents had passed away. My mother while she was giving me life and my father, years later, in a car accident. My aunt was my legal guardian, but I rarely talked to her. As of yesterday, she was across the country for a work trip, helping some poor man who was being accused of murder.

We lived in an apartment, two to be exact. We lived in the same building but our apartments were across the hall from each other. My aunt had fared well in life. Her job as a lawyer sustained us both and allowed us to live comfortably. She, bless her heart, believed in freedom and personal space, and she trusted me, which was something not a lot of kids my age could say about their parents, or whoever took care of them. I avoided talking about my mom as much as I could, but I knew that my mother, April Harris, had been an artist. My aunt used to tell me how she would paint every chance she got, even when she was younger. It was always fun for me to imagine a small human being with paint covered fingers next to a dilettante portrait of someone, but to my disappointment there were no pictures for me to compare my thoughts to. According to my aunt, my mother loved to paint the winter scenery, snowflakes and the like, specifically the month of November.

I had always laughed at that thought. How could my own mother love something that I despised so much? It made me sick knowing that I could never ask her, never meet her. My dad named me November. He said it had been in honor of my mom. I sometimes wondered if my mom had any other names already picked for me, and if she did why hadn't my dad used one of them to honor her? But, the name he'd given me had always made me feel special, until he'd died that is. After that it had just been a painful reminder that November was a horribly treacherous month.

When I was nine, so about eight years ago, my dad died in a car accident. It was winter and the roads had been slippery. I don't remember the moment when I found out. It wasn't like how they say it's supposed to be in the movies. I couldn't even remember if I was at daycare or at home with my aunt. It was all lost in a blur, sometimes it felt surreal. It was hard to picture my dad, even though I'd known him for nine years. Specific things about him had faded away over time. All I knew was that he was my father and he had loved me with all his heart.

I sighed, releasing a tired breath; and I gave the cold, metal door handles a hard tug and warmth immediately washed over me, like the tide of an ocean. I might not have liked the school but at least it was warm, an easy escape from the harsh weather that lurked outside the building.

"Hey, November," a few people greeted me somewhat cheerfully as I made my way down the hallway towards my locker. It surprised me how they could be so lively and buoyant in the morning, but I still smiled and addressed them back politely. I would never call any of those people friends, just people I had come to know over the years we'd gone to school together. They were more like acquaintances or associates.

My cold fingers hurriedly opened my locker—twenty five, two, fifteen—and I slid my backpack off my shoulders. Shrugging my heavy winter coat off, I reviewed my schedule, still getting used to the new one that I'd received a mere month and a half ago. It always seemed to take me a while to get used to my timetable and then by the time I'd memorized it, a new semester was starting and it was time to memorize a new schedule. However, change wasn't always a bad thing. It was good to have a little variety in your life, especially for someone like me who repeated the same boring thing day in and day out.

I had biology first and then calculus after, followed by a much needed spare hour, a study hall. When I chose my classes I should have dropped biology and taken another spare, which would've been the more logical option; but me being me, had to choose a course that was entirely useless. I didn't need biology because I wasn't going to become a biologist or a scientist. I knew what I wanted to be and I also knew that it had absolutely nothing to do with biology. Why did I need a science class to become an architect? I didn't, plain and simple like black and white. I sighed, pulling off my winter hat and placing it in the top part of my locker, casually glancing up and down the hallway to see if anyone was watching as I smoothed out my hat hair before I grabbed my biology textbook and slammed the locker closed.

My first classroom was on the opposite side of the school that my locker was on and I hated it. More walking, because like I said earlier, the school was big. It was three stories high and had almost a hundred and fifty classrooms. If you ask me, way more than was necessary for just seven hundred students. The exterior was simply creepy, able to steer newcomers away with just its looks. Correct me if I'm wrong, but I was led to believe that schools were supposed to be welcoming and friendly, given that students, teachers and staff were forced to spend a whole seven hours of each day in them. The walls were made out of brick, originally an off white color, but had stained a yellowish brown over time. The windows were gross, dead bugs and dirt covering the outsides; like they hadn't been professionally cleaned in years. Knowing the principal, they probably hadn't.

The interior had been renovated a couple years back and didn't match the outside at all. Inside, everything was brand new and clean, cutting edge materials and supplies. It was safe to say I liked the inside much better, not that I liked it though. When I arrived in class, I sat down at the back of the room by myself, as usual.

As soon as the bell rang, the teacher stood up and grabbed his list for attendance. I tuned out every name except for my own. "November Harris?" he called out tediously, his voice making it sound like attendance was the worst part of his day.

"Here," I said dryly as the few students who were actually listening turned to look at me. When he had finished, I mostly ignored his lesson because I didn't need to be here. I knew that I should listen still because, nonetheless, I didn't want to fail. A failed class didn't look so good on a college application. I told myself that every time I sat down in Mr. Adams' classroom, but I still couldn't bring myself to pay attention. I didn't seem to have that much willpower. I wanted to be at home drinking a nice warm mug of hot chocolate, sitting in front of the television and binge watching all my favorite shows.

I sighed and trained my eyes on the teacher as he walked around saying something that, no doubt, tied into biology.

My long, brown curls were pulled back into a ponytail, keeping the locks out of my face as I worked, and my forehead was covered in a sheen layer of sweat. I balanced the stack of dirty dishes on the center of my forearm, hoping they wouldn't tip to one side as I made my way back to the kitchen of the small diner I worked at part time. I seriously did not want a repeat of last week when I'd tripped over my own feet and went sprawling to the ground, smashing five plates in the process. I'd gotten about a dozen stares and a shard of broken glass had even managed to cut my hand along the side, but long story short it was not a pleasant experience and something I was trying so hard to avoid.

"Don't drop those, Clumsy," Joe, the man who owned the restaurant and my boss, said jokingly as he rushed by me with three plates of food. Clumsy had become my new nickname at work, the other employees preferring it over my real name. I rolled my eyes at him and pushed the large white kitchen doors open with my shoulder. The doorbells chimed signaling that another customer had arrived, but I was too preoccupied with my round of dishes to see who it was. I was afraid that if I threw even the smallest of glances behind me, I would lose my balance and risk dropping the plates.

I slid them carefully off my arm and onto the counter beside the sink where Shawn was hard at work, scrubbing them all clean for the next time they needed to be used. His short, curly brown hair bounced up and down as he furiously washed the dishes, an unexplainably happy glint in his green eyes. Shawn gave me a friendly nod as I grabbed the order for table seven, piling the food onto my sore arm. I smiled at Shawn, who always seemed to be in a good mood despite the fact that he did dishes all day long, and I walked back out into the dining room. "I've got table two," Jennifer, one of my co-workers, said to me distractedly and I bobbed my head at her, glancing to that section.

A man, I didn't know how old, was sitting by himself in one of the old, maroon-colored booths, facing me. His dark, curly hair was tucked beneath a red baseball cap, with a logo for a sports team I didn't recognize. The bill of his hat was pulled down in front of his face, obstructing his appearance from view. I turned my attention away from him and focused on safely delivering the food that was weighing down my arm, feeling relieved that my shift was almost over. The time I worked was the busiest part of the day. Around six o'clock in the evening the diner was always bustling with people every night, but by the time my shift was over, the number of people was significantly dwindling. There were only a few times that I could remember where I'd left in the middle of a big rush, leaving my co-workers to hope that my replacement came in fast.

As soon as I'd dropped off the order for the impatient family at table seven, I hurried back to the kitchen, already peeling away my apron before I'd reached the doors. I passed Jen on her way out to the dining room and she grinned at me cheerfully; but I could tell she wanted to get out of here just as much as I did. The loud buzz and clatter of the restaurant could be overwhelming at times.

"Is that for the guy at two?" I asked her in astonishment, gesturing to the pile of food she was somehow managing to carry.

"No," she laughed, nodding her head over to the large group of people who I hadn't even noticed come in. It looked like a family of five from what I could see, a mom, a dad, and three boys. "But speaking of him, could you drop his food off on your way out?"

I mumbled a quick yes, going into the kitchen to put away my unofficial uniform, shrug on my jacket, and grab the plate. The simple order of a burger and fries was waiting on the counter for Jen to grab them. I hung my apron on its hook before picking up the food. "See you," Shawn shouted and I waved with my free hand, saying my own farewells to him and Joe. I pushed my way through the swinging white doors and dodged the tables that were in the way as I walked over to table two, setting the plate down in front of the man. He muttered a thank you and slipped his phone into his pocket. "No problem," I answered, turning away quickly.

"You heading off?" he surprised me by speaking and I whirled back around to face him. His hat was still covering the majority of his facial features. I could just see his lips and chin, almost his nose.

"Yep," I chuckled awkwardly.

"Be safe," he said, his lips curving into a smirk. I hesitantly smiled back, mentally scolding myself for playing with one of the buttons on my jacket. If I kept twisting it, it was bound to fall off.

"Have a good night," I said, subtly excusing myself from the conversation.

"Thanks again for the food," he replied and I took that as an opportunity to exit the diner. The bells chimed on my way out, a sound that I was accustomed to hearing, and the cold air stole my breath in a white puff of smoke, making me glad that I had remembered to put on my coat.

The diner was a twenty minute walk from my apartment. I didn't mind the walk in the summer, but in the wintertime it could be uncomfortable. Nonetheless, I did enjoy the peace and quiet along my route. It was nice to be able to take the time to clear my head, breathe the fresh air, and just think about anything. I didn't mind not having a car like most of the other grade eleven students at my school. In fact, it didn't bother me at all. Even if sometimes I dreaded the very idea of walking. But hey, as long as I got where I needed to get, I guess I couldn't really complain.

My shoes made soft crunches as I walked on the gravelly sidewalk. I'd swapped my worn out winter boots for a pair of sneakers, which made navigating the busy diner much easier. Soon I would have to start bringing both pairs of shoes, unless of course I wanted my feet to freeze on the way home, which didn't sound too appealing. I shoved my hands into my pockets, wishing I had a pair of mittens, and kept walking, my feet floating across the ground.

The next day at school, after biology and calculus, I spent my study hall in the library. It was peaceful and quiet, but had ended all too quickly. Spanish class was next and I groaned. Spanish was my worst subject by far. I didn't know why I could excel at every other subject, but struggle so much with languages. However, it did let me know that learning French should be removed from my bucket list. In fact, taking Spanish class had pretty much drawn a large red X over the thought of speaking any languages that weren't English.

I entered the dimly lit classroom and made my way to the back. I always sat at the back in Spanish class, well most of my classes to be entirely truthful. In this room, the desks were small tables, one desk for two people but I sat by myself. I preferred to be alone rather than have to make small talk with a table partner. Plus, if I ever had to make small talk with someone in Spanish, I didn't know what I'd do.

The bell rang signaling the beginning of class. A few stragglers sauntered in a second after. The teacher fixed them with a cold glare as they hurried to their seats, and she began talking as soon as the classroom fell silent. No hushed whispers, rustling bags or restless feet, it was just a quiet room filled with high school students and a teacher with a loud, projected voice. It wasn't a moment after she had begun her planned lesson that she was interrupted by the door opening, creaking eerily on its hinges. You know that thing that every teacher does? When a person of higher authority, a.k.a. their boss, walks in and they immediately become a totally different person? That's basically what happened when Mr. Jones's face appeared at the door, poking his almost bald head through to look at the room full of students.

She impatiently turned to look but wiped the annoyed expression off her face when the principal walked in, smiling, suddenly cheerful. It was a drastic change from before, when her frosty gaze had swept fixedly over every student, carefully searching for any sign of electronic devices. Fortunately, my phone was safely tucked away at the bottom of my school bag.

She gestured for the two people who were at the door to come in and I, along with the entire female population of the class, curiously turned my gaze to the boy who trailed behind him. It was extremely odd for Brookhaven High to receive a new student this late in the semester, well, any time during the school year really. So naturally everyone wanted a look at the new kid on the block. Every girl in the room gave a small gasp. The oxygen all but vanishing from the room when they saw the boy's face, or rather what he looked like.

He was absolutely and utterly gorgeous.

His hair was black like the night at its darkest hour, curling behind his ears. His white short sleeved shirt hugged his upper body, showing off his lean muscular chest and perfectly sculpted biceps. His dark jeans hung low on his waist. I didn't need a close up to know he was hot and from what I could see, he was.

And he was alarmingly familiar.

I knew I'd seen him before and I racked my brain trying to think of where. The grocery store? No, plus he didn't look like the kind of guy who would shop for fresh fruit and boxes of cereal at the local shopping mart. He looked like he ate out every day, but never had to exercise a day in his life to maintain his figure. The apartment building? No, I rarely saw other people in the lobby and if I did it would be fairly easy to remember given its irregular occurrence. The diner?

My eyes widened as I realized he was the guy from the diner last night, the one who'd been seated at table two. I looked around the class curiously, trying to see if anyone here had seen him before, but judging by their reactions he was a complete stranger.

The way the girls in the room sat a little straighter and fixed their hair discreetly– although it wasn't– was more evidence that I had been correct. His gaze lazily swept the room and didn't linger on anyone. The principal made some apology to the teacher for interrupting her class, which she waved off quickly, and proceeded to introduce the boy.

"This is Ace Montego, he will be joining your Spanish class. Please welcome him kindly to the school," the principal said and quickly excused himself from the room. He wasn't very good at speaking in front of large groups of students, despite his role in the school, and it made laughter want to bubble out of me at the sight.

"Take a seat in an empty spot, Ace," the teacher said kindly, and I started mentally counting down the seconds until she dropped her friendly façade. It was bound to happen any second now and it was interesting to watch, plus it posed as a good distraction from everything else. But the way the room fell into a hushed silence made me feel the tiniest bit nervous and I glanced around the room quickly and gulped, realizing the only available seat was next to me. Just my luck.

I watched his face as he realized the same thing. His features remained impassive as stone, save for the slight curve of his lips as he smiled and made his way towards me. The smile didn't reach his eyes and I noticed that his nose was slightly crooked, as if it had been broken before, in a fight maybe? He reminded me of some of my peers who were those types of people, the kinds who got in fights and ended up in the nurse's office with sprained or broken body parts. I dropped my gaze to my desk, his empty expression sending chills crawling up my spine like spiders and ants.

"Hello," I heard in my ear, his breath fanning my neck. I shifted away from him unnoticeably and pivoted my body ever so slightly to face him.

"Hi," I said shyly, my voice quieter than his.

"I'm Ace," he said as he sat down next to me silently and I lifted my head up a small degree to look at him, remarking that his eyes were a shocking blue, dark almost black. I nodded, my eyes open wide in amazement, because I'd never seen eyes like that in my life, as I stared into his navy orbs. "And you are?" he grinned, starting my sentence for me, detecting my embarrassing loss of words.

"Oh, right. I'm November," I said, my face flushing red.

"November," he repeated, as if testing it out, investigating the way it sounded.

I waited for him to make some remark about how odd the name was but he never did. He stared at me as if it was my turn to speak, which felt like pressure to continue the conversation, and so that was exactly what I did. "Did you just move here?" I asked, for two reasons; the first one being curiosity and the second one because I'd felt like I had to.

"Something like that," he nodded vaguely and I smiled politely, accepting his bizarre answer.

"You were working at Joe's Diner last night, weren't you?" he questioned and I nodded stiffly, chuckling awkwardly, and then I inwardly cringed at the way my laugh had sounded. Have you ever said something and then wished you hadn't the moment after? Oh man, this discussion was basically one embarrassing thing after another.

"Yeah, that was me," I responded and he nodded, his gaze drifting behind me distractedly. "I almost didn't recognize you without your hat," I joked, attempting to get a laugh out of him.

"Hm?" he asked absentmindedly and I sighed, motioning to my head. "Your red hat," I mumbled, feeling like an idiot for having to explain my pathetic joke.

"Oh, yeah, my hat."

I turned my gaze back to the teacher and tried my best not to glance over at Ace. As the class went by, I could feel his gaze on me and it was extremely unnerving. I fidgeted nervously with my hands and squirmed in my seat, wishing that I could just sit still. "Are you okay?" he leaned in to whisper, a few minutes before the bell would ring.

"I'm fine," I said, a little annoyed at the amusement in his voice.

He sat back in his seat, crossing his arms over his chest, a smirk on his face.

"You don't look fine," he said quietly. I wanted to tell him that he'd get in trouble for talking but that would risk sounding like a two year old, so I stayed silent, pursing my lips and made sure I didn't move an inch for the rest of class, still as a stone statue. When the bell rang, I hurried to stand up but he was much faster. "See you tomorrow," he muttered almost rudely, walking by me. I stared after him as he made his way to the door that would lead him out into the hallway and furrowed my brow in curiosity as he stopped. Had he left something at the desk?

Right before he exited the classroom, he turned and locked eyes with me, dropping me a wink, then he left, disappearing out the door. Chills crept up my back and I shivered involuntarily. My cheeks tinged red and I looked around the room to see if anyone had noticed, and I let out a breath when I saw that no one was paying attention to me. That was the usual, though, why had I thought otherwise? I sighed and grabbed my books, fleeing the class, ready for lunch. Heck I was already ready to go home. School was such a drag. It made the days feel absurdly long when all I wanted was for them to go by fast.

I dropped my bag in the entrance way to my apartment and exhaled in relief. Another day was done. I slipped off my worn out black boots along with my hat and scarf, which were both coincidently a nice apple red color, and I unbuttoned my knee length winter coat and hung it up on the hook. I rubbed my reddened hands together, blowing on them repeatedly, in an attempt to warm them up. Making my way to the kitchen, I flicked on the lights. The apartment instantly illuminated and filled with a soft yellow glow.

The walls were painted pale blue, the color of the sky on a warm summer day. When my aunt and I had first moved into these apartments, the walls had an ugly musty green and rose with pink flowered wallpaper, an eyesore really. It had been absolutely horrid and my aunt had immediately set to work on getting the landlord to agree to ripping it down and painting. But, my aunt and I hadn't always lived in our apartments. We used to live in my old house.

My aunt was five years younger than my mom and between taking care of me and going to college to get her degree in law, she couldn't have afforded it yet. I was only nine so she had to pay someone to look after me when she was at school. We moved here last year and I liked this much better than the house.

I didn't remember a whole lot about my dad, but being in that house still brought back painful memories and the reminder that he was gone. I sighed, opening the fridge in search of something to eat. I would make myself some supper, then I would take a quick shower and do my homework. That way I would have the rest of the evening to relax and do as I please. I would probably end up doing what I always did when I didn't have to work; sit on the couch, mindlessly watching TV. Maybe I should ask Joe to make me full-time from now on. At least I would be making money in my free time. I nodded my head once firmly, settling on my plan for this evening. Who doesn't love wasting their time doing nothing?

# Chapter Two

I t was cold, which I had been expecting. It was the same as any other day during the godforsaken pre-winter in Brookhaven. Just plain cold and it made me dread the actual winter season that was fast approaching. I really wasn't having any of it.

I stared blankly out the window during biology. Anything and everything the teacher was saying going in one ear and out the other. I was too busy watching the first snowfall of the year, officially confirming that winter was here, to pay attention to the teacher. My excuses were getting worse as the days went by, but I shrugged, really not caring. The fluffy, white snowflakes that fell delicately through the sky were much more interesting than Mr. Adams' low, lazy voice.

But, biology was about to be over, which meant Spanish class was that much closer. Which meant Ace was that much closer. Which meant I was that much more nervous and more fidgety than I should have been.

I knew that I needed to calm down and get it together, but I felt like vomiting which was not a good thing. In fact, it was a very, very bad thing. Vomiting at school meant social suicide and I could not let that happen. Not that I had many friends, because I didn't, but I still made it by okay. I really didn't need or want to be the outcast of the school, to be that weird kid that everyone only knew because of something abnormal or embarrassing they'd done. I was happy just floating along, going with the flow.

The bell rang, yanking me abruptly from my thoughts and I scowled in annoyance. However, I did waltz out of biology class as fast as I could, heading to calculus. I liked math, contrary to the opinion of the majority of my classmates. It was practical, logical, and it was all numbers. Definitely my kind of subject. The math room, classroom number seventy five, was on the second floor, right beside the library where I would spend my study hall next period. It was the complete opposite of my biology classroom.

In bio, there were two large windows that filtered in sunlight, giving the room a bright and fresh complexion, which made people feel more awake and ready to start the day. It was a good room to be in, especially during first period where everyone was convinced it was the right time to catch up on missed sleep. Math, however, was in an unlucky room on the west side of the school. The morning sun was hidden behind the school, and the dank, drab color of the walls added to the ugliness of the room. I guess that the color of the walls really did have an effect on your emotions. I was still wondering when they would renovate this part of the building, pondering why they hadn't just done it all at once. Wouldn't that have been a huge money saver?

I sat down still, somewhat used to the wing of the school that hadn't been renovated, and pulled out everything I'd need. I glanced up at the small boxy window to my left and noticed a dead fly facing my direction, giving me the impression that it was looking at me. It was such an eldritch thing to see and I looked away quickly, but I knew that now that I'd seen it, I wouldn't be able to get it out of my head. It was like one of those mind tricking pictures, where there was a hidden double image and once you saw the other one, it was impossible to unsee it. I sighed, resting my chin on my hand as I tried my best to stare straight ahead to where the teacher would hopefully walk through the door soon.

Math was going to be a good distraction. It would be easy to get lost and completely absorbed in the problems and equations, the numbers and symbols. We were starting a new unit today and I was, hard to admit aloud, a little excited for it. My classmates would have pretty much shunned me or regarded me with the weirdest of looks, reserved for only the strangest things. I guess I was weird then because the new unit was probably going to the best thing I did all week. Yeah, my life was that boring.

As it so happens, it was a little bit too good of a distraction because I didn't even notice as the time flew by, quick as lighting. I felt jittery again as soon as the bell rang. I grabbed my belongings, my backpack and binder, practically running to the library for my study hall period. Perhaps being in a nice, quiet, calm environment would help me relax.

Wrong.

I spent the entire sixty minutes chewing on my nails, thumping my foot and wiping little beads of glistening sweat from my forehead. It was the most unproductive hour I'd ever had. Like I said, I really needed to get it together. As soon as I'd sat down in the library, I'd begun tapping my foot incessantly on the ground, the rhythm seeming to get faster and faster with every thump, and biting my nails. Since when did I do that?

Have you ever spent way too long just staring at nothing and worrying about something?

Well, I can officially say I have.

And so there I was, proving that worrying only made things come faster. Standing outside the Spanish classroom, my stomach was a bundle of nerves. All I could see was his gorgeous face winking at me as he walked out of the classroom. I was so close to ditching.

But as the bell rang, a wave of students pushed me into the classroom. I forced my legs not to freeze on the spot when I saw Ace already sitting at the table. I began making my way, slowly, over to my seat and I averted my gaze as he looked up at me. I stared hard at the floor, focusing on every scratch and every speck of dirt, just so I wouldn't have to look into his dark, unfathomable eyes.

I felt his excruciating gaze on my face as I sank down into my chair beside him, swallowing hard. I swear he could've heard my heart pumping in my chest, thumping loudly like the beat of a drum.

"Hey," he said, running a long, slender hand through his dark hair.

"Hey," I answered back, praying that he couldn't hear my voice shaking. Had it always been so hot in here? Or was it just me? It's just you, an annoyingly prominent voice chided in my mind. I almost yelled out loud for it to shut up.

"How's your morning been so far?" he asked and I gulped. How has my morning been? Well, thanks to you, Ace, it's been horrible. I was used to easy school days and relaxing nights by myself, not this nervous pit in my stomach and fingernail chewing. I swear I'd never done that before today. Why was I starting to pick up new habits all of a sudden? I groaned silently, everything feeling unanswered.

"A little boring, and kind of nerve racking," I admitted, laughing uncomfortably. Suffice it to say that was the understatement of the century.

"How so?" he asked and I was very close to slapping myself in the face. Why did I tell him that? I shook my head to clear my thoughts because boys weren't supposed to make me nervous. They had never made me nervous. It was a little bit frustrating.

Instead of looking at him, I focused my attention on the

wall behind his head. The old board was covered in posters, some in Spanish, others not, and ads for the school's extra-curricular activities. I used to be part of the debate team, until I quit because I'd felt like I didn't have enough time between work and school. I probably could have stayed on the team, participated in something, if I wanted to badly enough. I guess the problem was that I didn't want to.

"I have a test in English class later," I lied, without missing a beat, and I glanced up in time to see his eyebrow shoot up skeptically "Oh, really? What's on it?" he questioned and my mouth felt dry as I searched for another little white lie.

"Uh, it's about Shakespeare," I made up. That was believable, right? Shakespeare wrote plays and we were studying plays and literature, so to answer his question, yes, that was believable.

"Oh, interesting," he murmured and I pursed my lips, nodding slightly. "I think you're lying," he said suddenly, looking me dead in the eye for a moment before my gaze was pulled to his hand, which was twirling one of my curls around.

I opened my mouth to say something but found myself at a complete loss for words. My blood was rushing so fast and my head was starting to spin. I couldn't think straight. Clearing my throat, I pulled away from his touch slightly and he dropped his hand into his lap, letting my curl fall back into place.

My eyes traveled up his torso and then onto his face. I noticed with horror that he had just seen me staring at him, or, his body. A lazy smile curled the corners of his lips up and he smirked at me.

People like him got on my nerves. People who were so self-obsessed and narcissistic. I ground my teeth together and looked him dead in the eye. God, he was so annoying. He knew he was hot and he flaunted it. Everything must come so easily to him. "I have an English test," I said, my face lacking any emotion. He was not going to make me look like an idiot. I would not let him. I would convince him that I had an English test if it was the last thing I did.

"Hmm," he hummed softly, tapping his fingers on his leg. "I guess you'd know best."

I smiled smugly but my face dropped as he inched his chair closer.

"Don't look now but I think that blonde is checking me out," he whispered and I turned my head to look. Sure enough, Tiffany, a blonde with long luscious platinum curls and bright cherry red lipstick, along with every other girl in the whole classroom, was eyeing him up.

"You do know that every other girl in the room is checking you out, right?" I blurted. "Well yeah, except you," he said and I blanked.

"I was definitely checking you out," I said and then slapped my hand over my mouth. What did I just say? His grin reappeared on his face and he crossed his arms slyly.

"I know. I just wanted to hear you say it," he said and then chuckled at my horrified expression. I closed my mouth before I caught flies and narrowed my eyes.

"That was sneaky," I said, pointing my finger at him accusingly. He grabbed my finger and enveloped my whole hand with his.

"Pointing is rude," he said, flipping my hand palm up. I watched rather curiously while he traced the lines on my hands, like a fortune teller would. Something sparked in my head that maybe he was trying to read my mind and I pulled my hand back. His eyes narrowed for a second and he looked up at me. I flinched at the seriousness of his gaze.

His eyes were so dark, so blue. They looked endless, like I was staring into a bottomless pit. They were beautiful but haunting and I felt myself getting lost in them, blindly searching for something that wasn't there. The word 'capti-vating' came to mind as I stared at him and then I coughed awkwardly and looked away, tucking a curl behind my ear subconsciously. It was probably best that I started paying more attention to my schoolwork and less attention to him. Maybe he had the same idea because he didn't speak to me, not one word, for the rest of the class.

"Almost late," Joe muttered as I clocked in.

"What are you talking about? I still have exactly fifteen seconds! I might even take a walk or get some coffee," I said, grinning from ear to ear as he shot me a look that basically said "you better not".

"Relax, I'm kidding. What section am I on?" I asked as I skillfully tied my apron on, the small black piece of fabric with large pockets only falling to mid-thigh. In the summer, Joe provided us with full uniforms but during the winter he let us wear whatever we wanted under the apron. I'd worked here for as long as I could remember. I guess I'd started whenever I'd been old enough because it was hard to imagine not being here every second day for my part time shift.

"Take the first and fourth sections if you can handle it. If not I can take it. Jen called in sick," Joe said and I smiled softly, feeling bad because of how clearly stressed he was.

"Don't worry, I got it" I answered and he nodded gratefully.

"Thanks, you're an angel, Clumsy," he said as the door-bell chimed, the sound traveling out to us in the kitchen. I chuckled at the nickname as I exited the cooking area, heading straight for the table that was piled with dirty dishes. I could probably get those first and then grab the order for the person who just walked in.

"Can't a guy get some service around here?" I heard from behind me and I raised my eyebrows at the annoyingly familiar voice.

"Following me to work? Now that's just stalker-ish," I said without looking up and he laughed.

"Just getting something to eat," he said and I smiled to myself and reached over the table to grab the rest of the dishes. I had been right. He did eat out all the time. I turned around, the weight of the dirty plates making the muscles in my arm burn, and saw that he'd seated himself at the table directly behind me.

"I'll be right back," I said as I carried my load to the kitchen. "Where is Shawn?" I asked as Joe flipped a burger and I dumped the dishes into the sink.

"Late," he replied curtly and I sighed.

"Did you call Lisa or Daniel?" I asked hopefully and he nodded, but didn't look too happy.

"Daniel isn't coming and Lisa is on her way, but she's coming from her other job and might be a while," he said. I wiped my forehead, the thought of the nighttime rush already making me feel exhausted.

"Alright," I mumbled, more to myself than to Joe, and headed back to section one of the dining room where Ace was waiting. "Can I start you off with something to drink?" I asked and he nodded, his arms crossed over his chest.

"Chocolate milk," he said and I raised my eyebrow but wrote it down anyway. "What's that look for?" he asked, sitting forward a bit and I shrugged, sticking my notepad in my apron pocket.

"What look?" I asked and started to walk away, but he grabbed my arm.

"Sit with me," he said and I rolled my eyes at his ridiculousness.

"N! Let's get going!" Joe yelled from the kitchen, glancing

nervously at the large group of people who had just walked through the door.

"Can't," I said unapologetically to Ace, gratefully smiling at Joe, and twisting out of Ace's light grip. I made my way back to the kitchen. "Sorry, Joe," I apologized and he waved me off, taking two plates out to the customers.

I grabbed the chocolate milk quickly and dropped it off at Ace's table without even saying anything, and I hurried over to another table. Jotting down their order, I could tell that I was in for a very long night. I knew that I was going to pass out as soon as got home, and believe me, I was counting down the seconds.

*The wind whipped at my hair, long loose curls were plastered to my face, and the rain pounded down, soaking me from head to toe. I was shivering violently and my teeth clattered together, the chilliness of the air surrounding me. I staggered forward a few steps, pushing wet hair from my face.*

*"Nova!" A voice called, muffled by the wind and the rain. I spun around, searching for where the voice was coming from.*

*"There you are," I heard in my ear. An unmistakably husky voice said with obvious relief, "I was getting worried." I tried to look up to see who it was, but his face was obscured by the rain as he pulled his jacket off. It was leather and was probably what was keeping him warm.*

*I looked up from the jacket that he'd handed to me and gasped in shock. I stumbled backwards and dropped the jacket by my feet, throwing my arms out to catch me as I slipped.*

*"Nova," he murmured soothingly, dropping to his knees beside me. Something large and dark unfurled from behind him and surrounded us in a sort of cocoon like bundle, and I watched in shock and awe.*

*They were wings, huge black wings coming from his back.*

And then I woke up, gasping for air and covered in sweat. My white cotton bed sheets were tangled around my legs as I pushed my long, dark, curly hair back from my face. I fell back onto the bed in exhaustion. I felt like I hadn't slept a wink, then again all I'd been doing was tossing, turning and dreaming.

The sound of my front door slamming had my heart pumping and fear coursing through my veins. I pushed the covers off despite my instinct to curl beneath them, and stood up, slowly and quietly.

I felt the floor creak under my weight as I took a small step towards my bedroom door. My heart was pounding as I reached out to grab the handle, gingerly turning it. I opened it, going out into the hallway, and walking into the kitchen.

The darkness was haunting.

It sent chills creeping up my back and made the hairs at the back of my neck stand on end. It wasn't a pleasant feeling. A fear so pure that I was even afraid of the feeling itself.

Reaching out to flick the light on, I sighed in relief as my apartment was instantly flooded with light. My apartment was so familiar and it made me feel better, chasing away my inner demons. The clock read 3:42 and I groaned, knowing I wasn't going to be able to get back to sleep.

I'd gotten home late last night because I ended up having to stay an extra hour to help Joe out at the restaurant. Luckily, Lisa had come through and arrived as soon as she could, and had immediately set to work. I had barely been able to change into my pajamas once I'd gotten here. I'd just collapsed in a tired heap on my bed and dozed off.

I plunked myself down on the couch and grabbed a book, opening it to the page I was on. Humming softly to myself, I tapped my fingers on my thigh, bored out of mind. I felt tired, but if I closed my eyes I knew I would see dark black wings enveloping me.

It had felt so real.

Shaking my head to rid myself of those thoughts, I went into the kitchen to make something to eat, hoping it would distract me from that awfully bizarre dream I'd had. Eating was always a good distraction, for pretty much everyone.

By the time Spanish class rolled around, I was beat. I was so tired I really just felt like going home and sleeping. Even after getting in trouble for dozing off in biology and napping through most of my study hall, I was still tired.

I hadn't even thought of Ace as I'd walked through the classroom doors. Well, until I saw him. His presence was like a shock. It was as if someone had doused me with cold water. He smiled as he saw me, a lazy smile, and I watched as he leaned back in his seat, crossing his arms over his chest.

My gaze locked with his, but he looked away to his right. I stopped walking as I saw what he was looking at. A girl had taken a seat beside him, in my spot and I carefully watched him, gauging his reaction.

His smile disappeared and he leaned in to whisper something into the girl's ear which seemed to piss her off, seeing as how she got up and left. He looked back over at me and patted the empty chair, gesturing me over. I slowly made my way over to him, my drowsiness coming back. "You look exhausted," he said. I grumbled in response. Ace smiled again, dragging my chair closer to his.

I sort of pushed him away, moving my chair back. I wasn't in a very good mood and I was going to get angry if he started pushing my buttons right now. I wanted to be left alone. "Aw come on, don't be like that, Nova," he said into my ear.

That was all it took to wake me up. I sat up straight, my back stiff. What had he just called me? I found myself repeating the question out loud and he smirked. "I called you Nova."

"Oh, okay," I said, stumbling over my words. Nova. I started thinking about where I'd heard that name before, but Ace's voice interrupted me, completely jumbling my thoughts.

"You want to get out of here?" Ace questioned suddenly. It was spontaneous, it took me a moment to register his words.

"Um, no," I said.

"Why not?" he asked, sounding genuinely surprised. What, was he not used to girls turning him down or something?

"I barely know you," I answered, offering him the best excuse that I could come up with on the spot. Okay yeah, I talked to him on occasion and he sometimes showed up at the diner while I was working, but that didn't qualify us as friends. He was still pretty much a stranger to me.

"I won't hurt you, Nova," he murmured and I shook my head no. I really didn't want to go with him.

I turned abruptly away and focused on the teacher. Ace cursed under his breath but didn't talk to me again for the rest of class, which was probably a good thing.

As soon as the bell rang he was up and out of the class, without so much as a goodbye. I shrugged it off, packing up my books into my bag. I slung it over my shoulder and disappeared in the hallway, my stomach grumbling. I was glad it was lunchtime.

I was seriously considering leaving the school and going home to eat, but if I did, I'd probably end up not coming back for my afternoon classes. So what if I skipped one afternoon? I tried arguing with that annoying voice in my head but to no avail. That voice, no matter how small and insignificant, always won.

I got dressed for the cold Brookhaven weather and left the school that I hated so much, making my way to a diner on the edge of town. I probably shouldn't tell Joe I was helping out the competition, but they had really great food there, even if they didn't get as much business. I would eat at Joe's, but this other diner was special to me. It held memories.

My dad and I used to go there when I was little, but I hadn't been there in what felt like ages. I guess without my dad here there was no one to take me. Stopping myself from thinking about him, I focused my mind on other things. Other things being someone with black eyes and dark hair, and a smile that haunted my mind.

I shook my head and started walking, and after about fifteen minutes I arrived at my destination. I walked through the swinging door, the bell chiming as I pushed it open. The old diner looked pretty much the same as Joe's, but smaller. It had less seating and fewer staff. Inside were five wooden tables and seats with faded yellow cushions, light brown painted walls and a black and white checkered tile floor. I looked around at the few people who were inside.

There was one couple sitting at the table closest to the door and a man by himself with his back turned to me in the booth furthest from where I stood. He had dark hair and was wearing a white short sleeved shirt, a leather jacket balled up on the seat beside him. He almost looked like Ace.

And as if on cue, he turned and looked up at me, a wide grin stretching across his face.

Oh please God, no.

That was all it took for me to turn on my heels and walk straight back out the door I'd come through.

"Nova!" I heard him call and I felt his hand on my shoulder, halting my movement.

"Let go," I said.

"At least let me buy you lunch," he said, not threateningly at all. I looked at him suspiciously for any hidden motive but then decided that letting him buy me lunch wouldn't be the worst thing. After all, it was just lunch. I didn't ask how he knew I was going to be here, and I didn't ask how he'd gotten here so quickly. I refrained from asking him anything that I didn't want the answer to.

I nodded my consent and he smiled, grabbing my hand and hauling me back into the diner that I'd hurried out of. He pulled me back over to the booth he was at and sat down across from me.

I took my jacket off and stuffed my hat and mittens in my sleeve, a habit I was used to, and opened up the menu that was on the table. When the waitress came over to our booth, I was ready to order but Ace beat me to it. His knee brushed mine under the table.

"She'll have the burger, no onions no mustard, and the vanilla shake, oh and a side of fries," Ace said confidently and I looked at him in surprise. How did he know I was going to order that? I was ready to voice my question but he looked up at me with those shocking blue-black eyes of his and silenced me with his own question.

"That's what you wanted, right?" he asked, verifying what he already knew, and I nodded at the waitress, managing a smile. "Great, I'll have the same," he said and the waitress nodded, walking into the kitchen.

"How'd your English test go?" he mused, twirling a fork between his fingers.

"Wonderful," I mumbled, watching the muscles in his arms move. It was somewhat mesmerizing.

"Like what you see?" he asked cockily and my eyes jolted up to his, away from his arms. I blushed profusely, muttering a muddled response that he probably couldn't understand. He chuckled. His shoulders shaking softly as he leaned forward, steadying himself by placing his elbows on the table, staring intently at me.

"Are you happy, Nova?" he asked suddenly and my back stiffened at the question that had turned the mood in the room from playful to serious.

"Yes," I answered automatically. Who was he to ask me if I was happy or not? It was none of his business, I'd only met him, what, like three days ago.

His dark eyes watched me for a minute. His gaze so intense that I had to look away and squirmed awkwardly in my seat. I stared hard at the table, wishing that he would quit looking at me like he was a scientist and I was his new specimen. But even though he was angering me to no end with his serious questions and his smoldering gaze, I still stayed and ate lunch with him. I mean, after a few minutes he'd struck up a simple, lighthearted conversation that made it easy to forget about my earlier anger.

"Thank you," I said after, to Ace who had paid for my meal despite my protests.

"No problem," he said, shoving his wallet into his back pocket. We walked outside, both of us shrugging on our coats and I shivered as the cold air hit me.

"You going back to school?" Ace asked and I shook my head no. "What?" he asked in mock surprise. "The good girl is skipping school?" He held a hand over his mouth in fake shock and I rolled my eyes.

"I'm tired and I wouldn't be able to focus anyway," I mumbled my excuse, a little embarrassed that he'd called me out on it.

"Thanks again," I said awkwardly, stepping away from him in the direction of my house.

"I can give you a ride," he offered and trust me when I said it was tempting. A warm, heated car over this brutally cold weather? If anyone picked the latter, I would personally hit them. And so I vowed to punch myself in the face later because I shook my head no.

I wasn't getting in Ace's car. Doesn't every parent warn their kids about stranger danger? Seriously, come on. My parents aren't even alive and I still know the rule. Don't get into cars with people you don't know.

Eating lunch with him in a crowded–okay maybe crowded was a slight over exaggeration–diner had been one thing, but there was no way I was ever getting into his car, especially not today. "I'm going to walk. The exercise is good," I smiled politely and huffed, my breath coming out like a puff of smoke.

He rolled his eyes at my obvious and lame excuse but shrugged anyway. "Your loss," he said, turning and getting into his car. He drove a black Dodge Charger, which explained how he'd managed to get here so fast, and I fought the urge to laugh. Was everything this guy owned black except his t-shirts?

I sighed inwardly, turning back to the road that I would walk down. It would probably take me a good thirty minutes to walk back into town and to my house. Perfect, just perfect.

Shivering, I pulled off my coat and hat, tossing everything into a pile on the floor. I could have probably hung it up now and saved myself the trouble of having to do it later, but I was too frickin' cold. My fingers were numb and my ears were beat red, which was most definitely not a good thing.

Now that it was winter I think my opinion was biased because if I wasn't saving everything up for college then I would definitely get myself a car. Maybe I could say that now, but by the time buying a car actually rolled around, there was no way I would be able to go through with it. Besides, I needed all the money I could get, you know, college isn't exactly cheap.

I pulled my boots off my feet and peeled my wet socks off, throwing them into a corner. I made my way down the hallway and into the kitchen, turning on the light. I checked the thermostat quickly, deciding that the temperature wasn't absurdly low. I was just cold from walking home. I didn't turn the heat up.

If I did, I would forget to turn it back down and wake up in a pile of sweat, which clearly wasn't my favorite way to wake up, although it happened more often than not.

Chills crept up my back and I crossed my arms over my chest, hugging myself to warm up. Why did winter have to be so cold? I yearned for the summer months to come faster. It would be amazing to be able to go outside in shorts and a t-shirt without turning into an icicle in the cold weather.

I sighed. I guess I just had to deal with it like I dealt with everything, slowly and one day at a time.

# Chapter Three

My afternoon yesterday had been relaxing and wonderful. It was a well-deserved break in my opinion. I was always trying my very best at school, so taking a day off every once in a while was okay. Reviewing what I just told myself, I nodded firmly. If the teachers asked where I'd been, I had been at home with a very grave illness.

I sighed, flipping through the biology textbook I'd just been given. It looked like it would provide a massive amount of information and homework, so naturally I despised it. Just as the bell rang, the teacher called out for us to read the first chapter tonight and to be ready to discuss it tomorrow. Amazing.

Calculus was a breeze as usual, even though at the end of class the homework had really been piled on for tonight. I probably wouldn't be able finish it in time. I had a shift at the diner and I was praying that Jen had recovered from the flu, and that Shawn wouldn't decide to be lazy and not show up. Shawn was good at his job, when he actually came, and Joe wouldn't fire the only person who didn't hate dish duty.

I shoved the book into my school bag, and headed for the library. I had my study hall right now and I found myself sitting alone at a table, immensely bored. I tapped the eraser of my pencil on the table repeatedly, thumping my foot in time with it. I hummed softly under my breath and nodded my head.

I checked the clock quickly and groaned. It had only been thirteen minutes. If I started reading the textbook the time would go by faster, right? Oh you would never believe how wrong I was.

The seconds seemed to stretch into minutes that passed agonizingly slow. I knew that looking at the clock didn't actually make the time go slower because that was impossible, but believe me when I said that it felt like it. Watching the hand tick by one second at a time was excruciating. I shook my head, covering my mouth as I yawned, and adjusted my seating position. I was hunched over a table in the library, my study hall almost finished and my back aching, but I really needed to finish the biology assignment the teacher had given out today. It was supposed to be easy, but I just couldn't seem to grasp the concept.

So there I was, in Spanish class, sitting at my desk working on biology homework with a beautiful boy named Ace peering over my shoulder to see what I was trying so hard to figure out.

"I can help, if you want," Ace offered, seeing that I was struggling.

"You're good at biology?" I asked and I glanced at him doubtfully. Not to let stereotypes control my thoughts, but really? A pretty boy like him could not be good in school.

And boom, just like that, he'd proven me wrong once again. "I got an A in biology last year," he said into my ear and I inched away from him, feeling a little uncomfortable that his breath was fanning my neck.

"Then yes, I'd really like your help."

I was way too defeated to roll my eyes at the smug smile on his face as he moved his chair even closer to mine, grabbing my pencil from my hand. There was definitely not enough space between our heads as he explained what the question was asking and what I was doing wrong.

I had to fight every fiber in my being that wanted me to stare at him and force my brain not to turn to mush. He was actually really helping me with this, so listening to the words pouring out of his mouth was probably a good idea.

After a long ten minutes of him teaching me, I finally understood the project. "Thank you, thank you, thank you!" I exclaimed in relief and gratefulness, a little too loudly, because the Spanish teacher fixed me with a cold glare. I blushed when everyone turned to look at us and tried my best to ignore the amused expression on Ace's face.

We got a Spanish handout and I stared at it blankly, mentally face palming.

I swear to God every teacher had it in for me today. First biology, and we'd gotten a pile of calculus homework, and now Spanish? Seriously? I swear if my English teacher decided we should write a paper, I was going to be furious. I sighed, immediately getting to work on decrypting the language that was so foreign to me.

The tip of my pencil rested on a word that I didn't know, and I actually felt like throwing in the towel and giving up. "Date." I turned to Ace in surprise and sent him a questioning look. He nudged my pencil with his hand and repeated what he'd said. "It means date."

"Thanks," I said, looking back at the paper and writing a little note on top of it. I rubbed my eyes tiredly, because I didn't get as much sleep as I'd hoped for last night, and yawned. I kept writing down random Spanish words that sounded good together, hoping that they formed a legible sentence that the teacher could attempt to decipher.

"Hey, Ace," an extremely high pitched giggly voice said from off to my right somewhere.

"Hey," Ace said in acknowledgment, but he barely looked up at her, scribbling something down on his paper.

The poor girl looked baffled that Ace hadn't looked over and she blushed, fanning her cheeks. "I was wondering-," she started but Ace held a hand up.

"Could you give me a minute? I'm trying to work," he said, his voice sounding angrily impatient.

The girl mumbled something as Ace went back to writing and I looked over at him, catching his gaze. "That was so rude," I blurted out, and he looked at me, a ghost of a smile on his face.

"How so?"

"She is obviously interested in you, but you didn't even give her a chance-,"

"I've got my eye on someone else," he shrugged and I fell silent. Oh, then I guess he wasn't as rude as I thought, but he was still a little blunt.

"Okay," I shrugged and I caught him roll his eyes but I ignored it, turning back to my paper that was screaming my name. How joyful, who doesn't love Spanish homework?

"Hey, Clumsy. Glad to see you made it," Shawn said from the sink as I walked through the kitchen doors. I took a deep breath, smelling the familiar scent of burgers cooking on the stove, making my mouth water and my stomach growl.

"Me? You're the one who didn't show up," I laughed, peeling off my heavy winter jacket, switching it for my small apron. Shawn smiled sheepishly as I fixed him with a scolding glare, his cheeks heating up.

"Yeah, sorry about that," he said sheepishly and I shrugged. "Joe told me it was pretty busy," he said and I raised my eyebrows.

"You don't know how much of an understatement that is, Shawn," I replied seriously and he belted out a laugh, shaking his head as he went back to doing dishes. I shook my head a little as I grinned at Shawn's infectious laughter, hoping that my smile would also make Joe think I was really dedicated to my job. I supposed I actually was though. I was never late and I never called in sick unless I was deathly ill. Plus, I knew Joe had no intention of firing me.

I grabbed a notepad and dumped a few handfuls of change into my pockets, making my way out to the dining room. I glanced around and saw Jen, sighing in relief, and went over to section three where there were two tables filled with customers. "Hi, what can I get for you?"

And so it began. The superficial cheerfulness and the ear-to-ear smiles, carrying the delicious smelling food and the dirty, used dishes, walking back and forth from the kitchen and the dining room over and over again, all night long.

"Hey, Nova," Ace greeted me as I sat down next to him.

"Hey," I said softly. He was always here before me. It was like he waited outside the classroom for the bell to ring or his previous class was right next to this one. He moved his chair closer to mine and I made a small sound of protest in the back of my throat which he promptly ignored, as usual.

"How'd you sleep?" Ace asked, leaning lazily on our table.

"Good," I responded, narrowing my eyes in an irritated glare. He smiled a little and he lightly traced the bags under my eyes with his fingertip making butterflies erupt in my stomach, my skin tingling under his touch.

"That says otherwise," he murmured, referring to the dark under eye circles that seemed to be present on my face at all times recently. If anything was to blame it was biology class. Is lack of sleep and stress valid grounds to transfer out of a class? Probably, but I really shouldn't. I swallowed the lump in my throat and shook my head a little, clearing my thoughts.

I slapped his hand away, feeling suddenly annoyed that he could read me so easily. He chuckled quietly, glancing over at the teacher who had started talking.

"Go out for lunch with me," he said suddenly and I looked back at him quickly.

"I don't-," I started to say no but he pressed his hand over my mouth. My eyes widened in complete surprise and I pulled my face away from him.

"Please?"

I sighed and was preparing myself to turn him down when something in my mind clicked. This guy who was extremely gorgeous was asking me out on a sort of date. Seriously, what was wrong with me?

Well, despite the fact that he was an arrogant jerk, he was still really sweet when I thought about it.

"Sure," I agreed and his famous smile appeared on his face as he clasped his hands together.

"Great," he said, turning to look at the teacher.

"Where are we going to go?" I whispered discreetly as to not attract any attention.

"It's a surprise."

I sighed and grabbed my pencil, feeling like an idiot for agreeing to go out for lunch with him. One, I hated surprises. Two, I barely even knew him and I was about to voluntarily go with him somewhere? "I won't hurt you. You're safe with me," I heard in my ear and I stilled myself, finding it oddly weird that he knew what I was thinking again.

What I found even stranger was that I believed him. He'd said the words with such certainty and I trusted him, although I wasn't quite sure why. I would be safe with him and there wasn't any need to worry I told myself, folding my hands neatly in my lap.

Maybe I just needed to let loose and have a little fun. Yeah, that was definitely what I needed.

"This is what you had in mind?" I questioned disbelievingly.

"Mhm," he hummed softly, pulling into a parking space. He cut the engine of his car and opened up his door, climbing out. I did the same and carefully slammed the door closed, not wanting to damage the expensive car.

"We were here yesterday," I pointed out, unbuckling my seatbelt.

"But you like it here, yeah?" He asked to make sure.

"Yeah."

He smiled and held the door open for me, letting me walk into the diner, just like the last time we'd eaten lunch together. We sat down at the same table as yesterday and the same waitress— she probably worked the lunch shift—came up to us. She greeted us in a friendly matter and Ace ordered vanilla milkshakes to start. Oh how I loved vanilla shakes.

"Thanks," I said, clearing my throat quietly.

"No problem," he said, grabbing a menu.

"You want the same as yesterday?" Ace asked and I nodded slowly, remembering lunch from the previous day.

"How did you know what I was going to order yesterday?" I asked suddenly and he looked up at me, his dark gaze slicing into mine.

"Lucky guess," he said steely, his voice neutral. "Plus you seem like the kind of person who would order that," he added, shrugging his shoulders casually. That's bull. A lucky guess? Maybe for a psychic, and even that was a stretch because my order had been a fairly specific one. I shook my head to clear my thoughts and took a deep breath, watching as he shut the menu and slid it to the end of the table where the waitress could easily grab it.

"How old are you?" I asked even though the question was considered somewhat impolite.

He grinned crookedly at me and clasped his hands together on the table. "Eighteen," he answered and I nodded, waiting for him to ask me the same question. But he didn't, to my disappointment. Wasn't he curious? The waitress placed my shake on the table in front of me, the glass clinking against the wood as she set it down, and did the same for Ace.

"You ready to order?"

I listened to Ace rattle off the same thing as yesterday, and I watched him curiously. Wasn't there something else he'd rather have instead of what I was having? I mean, I'd met some people who were pretty fastidious when it came to their burgers.

Ace and I fell into an easy conversation about our futures. Well, it was mostly me talking about mine, and I sighed dreamily. I wished it would come faster. You hear all those people who say things like "enjoy life while you're young" or "don't grow up," but getting older was all I could ever think about, now and as a kid.

Maybe it was because my parents had died when I was young, or maybe I was just a complete weirdo, but I was so ready for life after high school. Life after this town.

"What classes do you have after lunch?" Ace asked and I groaned.

"English and history," I answered. I mean, I didn't completely hate the subjects but they were most definitely not my favorite classes. This semester was such a drag.

"I like history," Ace said and I looked at him like he'd grown another head.

"Why?"

"Because it's easy for me to picture myself there when everything happened," he said, grinning a little, and studying me for my reaction. I guess it was a plausible reason.

"That's cool," I answered lamely and he chuckled, his shoulders shaking softly.

"Here you go, enjoy your meal," the waitress said as she placed the two plates in front of us. I thanked her and so did Ace as we began to eat our delicious food. Joe was a better cook than the chef here, but for some reason I enjoyed eating at this place, even if it meant betraying Joe–in a sense.

Ace and I ate and talked. To my surprise, we got along surprisingly well. I barely even noticed the time flying by at a million miles per minute.

# Chapter Four

My shrill laughter sounded in the air, as other people's conversations buzzed around us. Ace chuckled also, running a long slender hand through his dark hair. "I still don't understand," I smiled, shaking my head.

Ace had been trying to get me to understand my biology homework. Thank God for his help, but I was a lost cause. I simply couldn't grasp the subject. Maybe that's because my mind was built more for numbers, not naming the parts of the human brain.

"That's okay," he said, leaning back in his chair. We were in Spanish class, sitting beside each other in the back row, like normal, and everyone else was turned towards their table partners, chatting animatedly. The teacher had given us a free period to do whatever we wanted, which was so completely unlike her, but I was not complaining.

"Why are you helping me?" I asked curiously, redirecting my attention to Ace.

"I can't help a friend?" he answered and I laughed a little, releasing a breath. Maybe he was just a good guy trying to help me out, yet for some reason, I couldn't bring myself to believe that.

Everything about Ace was a mystery. He had a sort of aura that surrounded him, and it made me feel like trouble followed him wherever he went. Or maybe not. Maybe he was the trouble.

I glanced up at the clock and watched it for a second. "Class ends soon," I pointed out, gathering all my books into a nice neat pile and then proceeding to shove them into my bag. I zipped it up. The thought of all my belongings spilling from my bag to the floor was utterly horrifying.

Ace held my pencil out for me and I tried to grab it without touching his hand, but our fingers brushed together making my spine go stiff. I sat up straight. My eyes opened wide at the sudden chill that had coursed through me. Goosebumps crept up my back and I pulled my hand away swiftly, pressing it against my leg to stop it from shaking.

Ace's smirk was present on his face and I swallowed, putting my pencil away in my binder. "Um, thanks for your help today," I stammered, my mouth extremely dry.

"My pleasure."

As the bell rang he stood up, offering me his hand. Not a chance, Ace. I stood up on my own, grabbing my books. I saw Ace roll his eyes but I ignored him and made my way out of the class, heading for my locker. I looked discreetly behind me and saw Ace strolling down the hallway, following me. I blew out a sigh and kept walking until I got to my locker, unlocking it and throwing my book bag in.

Ace leaned against the locker beside mine and watched me.

"Can I help you?" I asked, slamming my locker door. I supposed his intention was to be oddly cryptic. Even if he didn't mean to he'd succeeded wonderfully because of what he said next.

"Oh, if only you knew, Nova. If only you knew."

I groaned and rubbed my eyes, yawning. Sitting up, I glared

at the sunlight pouring through my window, bathing my entire room with a soft yellow glow. For a minute I sat there just staring at nothing, and then suddenly I jumped up.

Crap, I thought, I'd completely overslept.

I rubbed my eyes again sleepily and fell back onto my bed. Right, it's Saturday. I closed my eyes and thought about going back to sleep but eventually decided against it. I worked the lunch shift on Saturdays, starting at two o'clock, so I just had to make sure I arrived on time. Wouldn't want to accidentally pull a Shawn.

I climbed out of bed and padded over to my closet, searching for something to wear. I threw on an oversized hoodie and sweatpants. Not my best look, but oh well, it would have to do. I threw my hair up into a ponytail and made my way to the kitchen where I began to cook breakfast. Eggs and toast sounded absolutely delicious right now.

If only I was any good at cooking. I could remember the few times where I'd found a recipe online and tried to follow it, but every one of them had turned out to be a disaster, so I swore off cooking as to avoid any future mishaps like that. I settled on toasting a bagel and spreading strawberry cream cheese over it, something simple and easy and very hard for me to mess up.

A knock sounded at the door as I was setting the knife down and I stood up, brushing crumbs off my hands and onto the floor. I moved my plate to the kitchen island that I used instead of a table, and I went over to the entranceway, smoothing down my hair as best I could.

I threw open the door and had to force my jaw not to fall open in shock. "Well don't you look lovely," he smirked, leaning against the door frame. I stumbled over my words and crossed my arms over my chest self-consciously. "What are you doing here?" I demanded, his presence sparking my temper.

"We're going out," Ace said and I shook my head.

"Uh, no. We're not. And how did you find out where I live?" I asked.

"School records," he shrugged and stepped inside the house. I was pretty sure that he was not allowed access to those, although I was a little bit curious as to how he'd managed to obtain them.

"I didn't say you could come in," I said angrily, shaking off my curiousness and followed him into the house.

"But you want me here." He flashed me a smile and tucked a loose strand of hair, that hadn't made it into the ponytail, behind my ear.

He turned and looked at my cream cheese covered bagel sitting on the table, waiting for me to eat it, as I stared at him, my eyes narrowed into slits. "That looks gross," he remarked, almost rudely, grabbing the plate and dumping it in the trash.

"Hey!" I protested, lurching forward to stop him.

He chuckled and pushed past me gently, going into the fridge and pulling out some food, the limited supply I had. "Ace, I really-" I started but he cut me off with a wave of his hand.

"I'll cook you something to eat," he told me and I found myself nodding in agreement. "Wouldn't want you to die of lack of proper nourishment or food poisoning," he shrugged, his sentence seeming to take an unnecessary dark turn.

"Uh, okay. Let me go, um, freshen up?" I said but it came out sounding like I was unsure, like I was asking a question. I sighed because I had too many unanswered questions these days.

"Why? You look pretty good in that sweater," he said teasingly and I chuckled, rolling my eyes at his idiocy.

"Be quiet," I muttered, walking out of the kitchen.

"I'll be right back," I tossed over my shoulder, hurriedly

going into my room in search of something nicer. Something more presentable to wear.

I hit my head against the closet door, groaning. Really Ace? You just had to show up out of nowhere and sweep me off my feet? I sighed and pulled a blue crop top over my head and put a pair of black jeans on, then a red plaid cardigan over top. Whenever we decided to leave, my clothes were going to be covered by my heavy winter jacket anyway, but I still liked to be well dressed underneath my outer attire, just in case. Better, I thought. I mentally prepared myself to go out into the kitchen where Ace was waiting patiently and cooking me breakfast.

I was about to step out of my room and then stopped abruptly, catching a glimpse of myself in the mirror I had hanging on my bedroom wall. I quickly let my hair down, finger combing it into place, and then gave myself a nod of somewhat-approval.

I walked out into the kitchen and saw Ace eyeing the stretch of exposed skin on my stomach. I rolled my eyes and sniffed at the delicious smell of food that was cooking. "What is that?" I breathed in deeply, smelling the air.

"Eggs and bacon," he grinned, turning back to the stove. It smelled heavenly and my stomach growled in anticipation.

I floated over to him and stood on my toes to see over his shoulder. "Go sit down," he said gently, turning me to face the table. I took a seat on a chair and twisted around to watch him cook. He put a plate down in front of me, completely distracting me, and I thanked him gratefully. "Eat up, we have plans," he said, watching me take a bite of the food. It was ridiculously amazing. It almost made me forget to object his statement.

"I'll hang out with you, but I have to be at work by two," I said and he nodded, but sighed dramatically, checking his imaginary watch.

"That only gives us three hours," he pouted and I laughed, taking another bite of the food.

"Thank you," I said again, mumbling around the food in my mouth.

"No problem."

As soon as I was done eating, I put the plate in the sink and rinsed it off with water quickly, wishing I had Shawn here to take care of the growing pile of dishes that were sitting, yearning to be cleaned. It was puzzling how Shawn could like doing dishes that much.

"Ready to go?" Ace asked, coming up behind me.

"Uh yeah, quick question, though," I said as Ace pulled me out the door, barely giving me enough time to lock it and grab my jacket. "Shoot."

"Where exactly are we going?" I asked and he grinned, smiling smugly.

"You'll see," he said and I sent him a murderous look.

"Really? You're not going to tell me where we're going? What is with you and surprises?" I asked and he laughed, his chest shaking softly.

"I have a right to know," I added, prepared to list off a bunch of reasons as to why he should tell me, but saw that he wasn't going to listen and let him drag me to his car. I got in the front seat and buckled my seat belt, leaning back.

What was up with Ace? Something seemed off about a gorgeous guy showing any interest whatsoever in me. "You look like you have a question for me," Ace remarked and once again, it surprised me that he knew what I was thinking.

"How come you're-," I cut myself off, searching for the right words. "Why are we doing this?" I asked and he looked at me with a glint in his eye.

"You're going to have to elaborate," he said, but for some reason I felt that he knew exactly what I was asking, he just didn't want to answer. But right now I didn't really care if he wanted to change the subject. I wanted him to answer my question truthfully so I could figure out what his intentions were.

I pursed my lips and tried again.

"Why are you hanging out with me? Obviously you have some sort of motive," I said and he raised his eyebrows. I stared into his cold and calculating eyes, trying to read him like he read me, but failing miserably. He was as much of a mystery to me as ever.

"Well look at you. You have everything figured out," he said, smirking smugly, like he knew something I didn't. "Why is it so hard to believe that I just want to hang out with you?" he asked after a while of silence and I rolled my eyes.

"Because, it just is."

"Explain."

"You could hang out with any girl in the school. All of them would jump at the chance. So why me?" I asked and he turned to look at me, his eyes as dark as hell.

I watched curiously as he pulled over, stopping on the side of the road. He got out of the car and came over to my side of the car, opened the door and yanked me out- but gently still.

"I like you, Nova. You're not like the other girls. I need you to trust me," he said and I watched him with wide eyes.

"Trust you? I barely know you! You know exactly what I'm thinking all the time and you just show up at my house randomly with no explanation?" He didn't say anything so I continued with my angry, confused rant. "Who are you?" I demanded and he leaned into me, bracing himself with an arm on either side of my head. His eyes found mine and I watched as his pupils grew bigger, and for some reason, I couldn't stop staring at those insanely dark orbs.

"My name is Ace Montego. I'm a regular guy that you met in Spanish class at school. I like hanging out with you because I have a crush on you," he said and I nodded, agreeing with him although I didn't know why. "And you trust me," he said, putting a space of about three seconds between each word.

"I trust you," I repeated and he nodded, pushing away from me.

"Good," he said, clasping his hands together, something he seemed to do often. "Now let's go," he said, helping me back into the car. My head started pounding as soon as I sat down, and I massaged my temples with my fingers, slowing my breathing.

Ace started the car and pulled away from the curb, his eyes set on the road in front of him.

"What are we doing here?" I asked, looking over at Ace skeptically as we arrived at our destination, and then turned my attention back to the building in front of me. It was tall and made of brick, a dull red color, and had a large faded sign across the top of the doors that read the name of the... restaurant?

It sounded like it was a restaurant, but it didn't really look like one.

"Don't judge it yet," he laughed, knowing what I was thinking. Maybe he could read my mind, or maybe he could see the disgusted look on my face and tell that I was harshly judging the unfamiliar place. I mean, if I was going to eat anywhere it would be at Joe's or the other diner, not this trashy looking place.

I rolled my eyes and walked through the doors, glancing around. The lighting wasn't very good in here but from what I could tell, it was dirty and drab. Maybe I was just biased. After all, I did work at a popular, busy restaurant.

Gross, I thought, running a hand over a table and inspecting it for dust. Surprisingly, it was clean. Ace folded his hand over mine and pulled me close to him. "What are you-?" I started but he shushed me, gently placing a finger in front of my lips.

He gently pushed me back against the wall and leaned into me, his body pressing against mine, stealing the air from my lungs.

"Be quiet," he murmured into my ear. If anyone else was even here, they would probably think we looked like idiots. But judging by the absolute silence that hung in the air around us, we were alone. The thought sent both chills crawling up my back and butterflies flying in my stomach.

He stared straight into my eyes, his face getting closer to mine. My breath hitched as his lips neared mine and I feigned boredom, hoping he hadn't heard my uneven breathing.

"Kiss me."

"What? Why?" I questioned, not lowering my voice despite the fact that he'd told me to be quiet. This place was clearly deserted, anyway, so it wasn't as if anyone would hear me.

"Nova," he muttered and Ace kept his hands cupping my cheeks and pulled my face to meet his.

"I'm going to do it," he told me and I bit my lip. Would kissing him really be that bad? It was just one simple, harmless kiss. I started to lean closer, not really thinking about the possible consequences, just knowing that I wanted this to happen. Too bad we never actually got to the kissing part.

# Chapter Five

"Ace?" A deep voice said and Ace cursed under his breath, turning around. He stood in front of me as if he was hiding me from the person he was facing, which of course only made me curious.

"Ah, Darrius. I didn't know you were here," Ace said, running a hand through his hair. I stepped out from behind Ace to see who was there and the guy's eyes focused on me.

He was tall. He probably had a good five inches on me and at least one on Ace, and his skin was tanned. His eyebrows were thick and dark like his wild, spiky hair and his lips were wide. His jawline sharp. His features looked brooding, like he was angry, but he couldn't be, he seemed more... surprised?

He was regarding me with wide eyes.

"It feels like it's been forever," he muttered, staring right at me, although he was obviously talking to Ace because I had surely never met this person before in my life. His face didn't hold even the slightest bit of recognition, so I shook it off and decided not to let it bug me.

"And who's this?" he asked, but his voice held a hint of something close to sarcasm, stepping closer. "No one, Darrius," Ace said, turning to look at me and I chuckled. If

Ace wasn't going to introduce me to his friend then I was definitely going to introduce myself.

"Hi, I'm November," I said, waving a little and shaking off the annoyed look Ace sent me. My voice sounded so small in comparison to the two boys whose voices were much louder and deeper. Darrius's jaw hardened and he clenched his teeth, but his expression remained one of amusement.

"Nice to meet you, November. I'm Darrius," he said, crossing his arms over his chest, making his biceps bulge.

My gaze flitted over to Ace who was watching dryly, seeming annoyed. No, annoyed wasn't the right word. Ace was pissed. A frown was present on his face. His lips turned down into an evident scowl. "Nova, let's go," Ace murmured in my ear quietly, placing a hand on my hip.

"Already? We just got here," I pointed out and Ace clenched his jaw, clearly not having wanted me to bring that fact up.

"Yeah, Ace. Why don't you stay a while?" Darrius said tauntingly and I looked over to see what he would say. Darrius and Ace locked into a silent staring contest as if they were speaking to each other through their minds, and all I could do was watch.

"No, we're leaving." Ace decidedly grabbed my hand and pulled me away from the wall, pushing past Darrius. As we passed, my gaze locked with Darrius's and I gasped inaudibly, surprise hitting me like a moving vehicle; and not just a small car, more like a giant monster truck.

His eyes were pitch black, darker than the night, darker than Ace's eyes by a lot, if that was even possible. "See you around," he said, turning away swiftly and walking back into the backroom, most likely the kitchen. I still wasn't entirely sure if this restaurant was still in business but I suppose it didn't really matter. Ace didn't seem like he had any intention of sitting down for a meal with me right now.

"Ace, slow down!" I called, struggling to keep up with him, pushing the door that he'd let fall shut. His legs were longer than mine, given that he was much taller, and his strides were double mine. I was practically jogging.

"Sorry," he said curtly, coming to a stop once he realized that I was having a hard time catching up with him. He turned to face me and I jumped away from him in alarm, stricken with fright.

"What the heck?" I said when I looked at his eyes that weren't their usual mesmerizing blue. They were glowing, and not in the metaphorical way. They were red, bright red. My mouth fell open as I watched him, and it only took a moment for his face to light up with understanding.

He turned away, his hand flying up to his face to rub his eyes and I stood there, trying to breathe normally. I noticed him tilt his head back in exasperation or concentration—I couldn't tell which—and heard him curse under his breath. When he turned back, his eyes were normal, a beautiful dark unfathomable blue. "What just happened?" I said, pulling my hand away to avoid his touch. "Explain to me, right now," I demanded, anger and confusion mixing together.

"Hey, stop. Look at me," he said, grabbing me by the shoulders. Terror coursed through me at the small touch and I had to restrain myself from letting out a loud ear shattering scream.

"Let go!" I yelled, twisting in his grip, panic filling my chest.

"Look at me," he repeated, his voice slow and calm.

He took my face in his hands and forced my eyes to meet his, and I cringed away, half expecting to see frightening red orbs looking back at me.

"Forget that," he said, our eyes locked together. My mind, that had been racing before while it searched for an explanation, began to slow, becoming sluggish with every passing second. "My eyes are dark blue almost black and they have always been that color."

I blinked once in confusion and Ace let go of my shoulders, crossing his arms over his chest. "What are we doing out here?" I asked, not quite sure why I was breathing like a runner after a five mile marathon.

"Fresh air," he said simply, leaning against the wall. My thoughts wandered to when we were in the store, what was about to happen before Darrius walked in. He was going to kiss me, and I was going to let him.

My cheeks flushed pink, which he obviously saw in the midday sun, because he smirked at me and pushed himself away from the wall. "Nova," he said, pulling me close. "You want to pick up where we left off?" he asked and I seriously considered it.

Don't ask me why, because I really don't know, but I shook my head no. His smile disappeared and his gaze hardened, but he didn't say anything. He simply pulled away and guided me gently over to the car, helping me in. "I have to go to work," I said, even though I was sure I would arrive an hour and a half early if we went now.

I flinched as his car door slammed shut loudly and he started the vehicle, pulling out of the parking spot his car had been in. "I'm sorry," I mumbled, not sure what I was apologizing for. But I knew he was angry or annoyed, and it was something I'd done or said. I turned my head to the side, looking out the window as I waited for his response.

"It's fine, Nova. It's your loss, anyway," he said harshly and I bristled in anger.

"Excuse me?" I asked, offended by what he'd said.

"How often does a girl like you get to kiss a guy like me?" He asked rhetorically and I gaped at him, his words angering me at first. They would hurt later. He realized his mistake and he looked at me apologetically, but it was too late. I was far too mad.

"Stop the car," I said, clenching my jaw and grinding my teeth together.

"Nova, I didn't mean that–,"

"That's great, Ace. And guess what? I don't care. Stop the car," I interrupted and he shook his head no.

"Not happening," he said, pushing the car to go faster on the road.

"Fine, have it your way," I said, staring at him fiercely, pulling the door handle.

The door swung open with a sudden force and Ace's eyes widened in alarm. I struggled to keep my gaze locked with Ace's as the door tried to fully swing open, the strength of the wind being too much. He slammed on the brakes and the car came to a screeching halt, allowing me to safely climb out. I shut the door angrily and started walking down the street. My knee length coat was making an annoying crinkling sound as I took each step further away from Ace, and it wasn't helping my mood any.

Brookhaven wasn't a big town, I would be able to get to Joe's within twenty five minutes. He'd even be happy when I arrived an hour early for my shift.

"Nova!" Ace called after me but I ignored him. He yelled my name again and still I kept walking stubbornly, making him frustrated.

"November," I heard right in my ear and I jumped at his sudden closeness. I yelped as he picked me up and threw me over his shoulder, turning back to his car.

"Ace!" I yelled, hoping that he'd get mad at me for yelling into his ear and put me down.

It was the middle of the day, the sun was high in the sky, and yet there was nobody around to help me? God, I hated small towns. This one in particular. He dumped me in the passenger seat, closing and locking the door with the key, and climbed back into the driver's side.

I sat in the front seat of Ace's car, my arms crossed over my chest and a frown on my face. He smirked at me occasionally, looking over. "I wasn't going to let you walk," he informed innocently, like he hadn't done anything wrong.

"I don't see why not," I retorted, inspecting the glass that had become particularly more interesting than he was.

"It's a thirty minute walk!" he exclaimed and then mumbled something under his breath. He shook his head dismissively when I turned to see what he'd said. I huffed and leaned back against the seat. "Look, Nova. Let me explain," he said, referring to his snarky comment earlier. He scratched his head, his Adam's apple bobbing as he swallowed nervously.

"I was embarrassed that you rejected me so I lashed out." I still wasn't having any of it and he groaned, licking his top lip once. He needed a better excuse than that to make up for his rudeness. "I don't really do the whole confessing feelings thing—although I guess I'm doing that right now—I don't know, Nova."

He ran a hand through his mess of curly black hair and I sighed, giving in way too easily. What can I say? I was a sucker for cute boys. "Nobody else makes me this—this confused and flustered," he said admittedly and I smiled a little at him, as his cheeks reddened in embarrassment.

He sighed, watching the road while tightly gripping the steering wheel with his right hand. He glanced over at me and saw me holding back laughter. His mouth fell open in mock anger as I giggled and he rolled his eyes. "Yeah, because it was so funny," he said sarcastically and I nodded in agreement.

"It really was," I chuckled and he glared at me. "But I forgive you," I said eventually and he smiled in relief, turning a corner. We sat in a comfortable silence as he drove the rest of the way to Joe's Diner, pulling up in front of the old restaurant. "Thanks for today, Ace. I had fun. See you at school," I said, waving a little as I got out.

He laughed a little and rolled down the window to talk to me, seeing as I'd already slammed the car door closed. "At school? What about tomorrow?" he questioned light-heartedly and I stared at him, baffled.

"Don't you have stuff to do or something?" I said and he shook his head no, grinning slowly.

"See you tomorrow," he said as he stepped on the gas, pulling away from the diner.

"I have other things to do!" I shouted uselessly at him as his car sped away. I shook my head, smiling inwardly.

As I made my way inside, I recalled meeting Darrius in the restaurant and almost kissing Ace just moments before he'd walked in. The thought of kissing Ace made butterflies erupt in my stomach and I blushed, my cheeks tinged red.

What a day, I thought to myself.

"What the hell?" Joe muttered to himself, putting the plates down on the main counter. He proceeded to walk over to me, a look of utter concern on his features. I honestly thought something was really wrong.

"What?" I asked, my heart dropping worriedly. He grasped my face in his hands, staring dead at me, the creases around his eyes appearing as he tried to hide his smile.

"Are you okay?" he demanded and I nodded slowly, looking at him awkwardly.

"I think so, why?" I asked and his lips curved up into a playful smile. I raised my eyebrows questioningly when I saw that it was some joke he was about to make. Most likely at my expense. I knew Joe all too well.

"You're an hour early," he said in fake astonishment and I rolled my eyes, pushing his hands away. He grinned and let out a hearty laugh.

"Leave me alone!" I laughed, making my way to the back to start working.

"Don't forget your apron!" he called after me and I held my hand up over my shoulder, signaling to him that I'd heard and I would remember.

It was Sunday and Ace had taken me to the library to work on my biology project. To be precise, his exact words were, "Because you probably need my help. I mean, who wouldn't?" I'd rolled my eyes but had let him take me to Brookhaven's public library.

The town's public library was definitely one of my favorite places by far. It was big and spacious, bookshelves lining row upon row and each one stacked with books, all the way to the top. It was old and there was never anyone who wandered all the way to the back, well, except me.

Ace had to leave soon though, or rather, any minute now. His friend Charles was coming to get him, and he had described him briefly to me upon mentioning his name. Apparently, Charles was a blond jokester. He was easy to like but could be quite dumb at times, and he was the biggest player on the planet.

Ace had annoyed the crap out of me this entire day and I was almost looking forward to him leaving. And yet somehow we'd ended up here, standing close to each other near the tall bookshelf at the very back of the library. The things that happened when Ace was around would never cease to amaze me.

"Nova," he murmured, holding my face in his hands. He leaned in close, his mouth almost touching mine.

"Ace," I said his name back, but I had probably sounded a bit annoyed, maybe a little desperate for him to just kiss me already. What was the point of rejecting him at this point? Besides, it'd been a while since I'd kissed anyone.

The corners of his mouth turned up in a grin. "Someone's impatient," he said and heat crept up my neck, my cheeks burning. He laughed softly and tucked a lock of curly brown hair behind my ear. I gazed up at him and his eyes flitted to my lips. My breath hitched in my throat as he walked me backwards, up against the bookshelf. He flashed me his trademark smile and brushed his lips against mine.

"Ace," I demanded, lacing my fingers around his neck and pulling his mouth down to meet mine. His perfect lips pushed mine apart gently and his hands cupped my cheeks. The way he kissed me was in a way that was so gentle and sweet. I had a hard time believing it was Ace kissing me.

I had never seen this side of him before. He hid behind his cold and heartless exterior so well, I doubted anyone else had either. His mouth stopped moving but his lips hovered in front of mine for a moment while I drew a shaky breath. When he pulled away more, my lips felt tender and swollen, as if they had just been battered. He used his thumb to gently caress my cheek and his dark blue eyes stared back at me, studying me.

"Ace? You here?" someone, presumably Charles, yelled loudly from the isle. His footsteps sounding closer by the second as he searched through rows of bookshelves.

"Yeah," Ace called back, his eyes never leaving mine as he did. He backed up slowly and disappeared around the corner, removing himself from sight. I ran a hand through my hair, pushing it out of my face, and did my best to slow my breathing.

I stared at the spot where Ace went and my heart swelled with happiness, but my mind clouded with confusion. He'd told me that he liked me but he had been joking, I was sure. Maybe he does actually like me, or maybe he doesn't.

Maybe he was just being a jerk and playing with my feelings.

I sighed and pushed my hair out of my face again and sunk down into my chair at the table, grabbing a biology book from where it was sitting on the table.

It made me mad that Ace was growing on me and that I was starting to like him. He was so full of secrets and lies, and I didn't know how I would ever be able to trust him.

Whatever, I thought. Who cares?

# Chapter Six

Nervousness pooled in my stomach as I stood outside the Spanish classroom. I'd tried to take deep breaths to calm myself but it hadn't worked. Not that I'd expected it to.

Ace and I had kissed at the library yesterday and to be completely honest, I wasn't really sure how to act around him now. What if he acted like nothing happened? The thought was terrifying and I gulped, trying to take a long, deep breath.

I forced my feet into action and walked into the classroom, keeping my eyes trained on the floor. I cursed myself repeatedly when my heart rate accelerated as I felt Ace's eyes on me.

I didn't even need to be looking at him to know he was looking at me. I could feel his intense gaze as I made my way towards him. I was walking through the many rows of desks when someone's foot shot out right in front of my feet. Well, crap.

I stumbled and dropped my books on the ground as my hands flew out to catch myself before I hit the floor. Not that I needed to, though. Someone's arms went around me and caught me, to my surprise. I looked up at my savior, completely breathless, and saw Ace staring down at me.

"Are you okay?" He asked quietly as I smoothed out my hair. His face held a look of concern, which was strange for someone like him, and I nodded a little as he let go of me after making sure I was able to stand. His expression morphed into something close to anger as he turned towards the guy who'd tripped me. I furrowed my brow in confusion when I saw it was Shawn.

Shawn? He wasn't that kind of person. He was nice and sweet, helpful and honest. And besides his character really shouldn't matter in this situation because he and I were friends. We'd worked together for a few months now. We weren't best buddies by any means but he was still my friend, and that should count for something. Right?

"Do you have a problem?" Ace asked him and he mumbled an incoherent response. "What was that?" he asked, placing his palms on the desk and leaning forward. Shawn stared straight down at his desk, refusing to look up. "We can take this outside, if you'd prefer," Ace hissed, so quietly I almost hadn't heard him.

He looked up then at Ace and gave him a once over, considering his offer. "Yeah, sure," he said confidently, pushing his chair back.

"Ace, its fine, really I–" I started but they were already out the door. I glanced between my books and where the two angry boys had just gone and decided to follow them, leaving my possessions scattered on the floor and ignoring the curious onlookers and the fixated glare of the teacher.

I chased after them and apparently they were remarkably faster than me because by the time I found them outside, they were already angrily shoving each other.

Shawn was bigger than Ace, but Ace looked like he had more experience as he easily dodged blows and hits that were coming his way. Shawn, on the other hand, wasn't as lucky. He took two punches to the jaw and one to his stomach before he doubled over, yelping in pain each time Ace's fist came in contact with his body.

Ace backed him up to the wall, his eyes narrowing at my co-worker who'd tripped me, but I was fairly certain Ace didn't know that I worked with Shawn. Ace was seething. He looked like he was going to turn into the freaking Hulk and crush everything in his path in the process.

"Leave her alone, Darrius," I heard Ace hiss as he shoved Shawn against the brick wall of the school. Darrius? That was Shawn. I of all people knew that. He spit something back in response to Ace who then proceeded to punch him in the face. "Get out," Ace demanded, punching Shawn again. He repeated the same thing as he hit the poor kid again, harder each time. I watched in shock, unable to move, as blood slowly ran down his face, faster and faster each time he got hit.

"Ace!" I screamed at him, yelling for him to stop.

Ace let go of him and dumped him on the ground, leaving Shawn hunched over against the wall. "Oh my god," I said, covering my hand with my mouth, attempting to run over to him. "We have to help him–" I started to say but Ace grabbed my arm.

"He's fine but we need to leave," he said, pulling me along by my wrist. His hands were cold and hot at the same time, a perfect mix between the two. His hold on me was strong and it was going to take all my might to weasel my way out of this one.

"Leave? No," I answered, tugging my limb out of his grip, stumbling back a step or two as he let go.

"Nova," Ace said forcefully, turning to look at me. "We're leaving," he said again, slowly this time as if it would help him get his point across to me.

"What if I don't want to?" I countered, crossing my arms over my chest in annoyance. He could not just order me around and expect me to obey him, to do exactly what he wanted all the time.

"You don't have a choice," Ace said, shrugging. "We can do this the easy way or we can do this the hard way," he informed me and I glared at him.

"You can't make me leave. I have to go to class, Ace. I need to get my books and I need to–,"

"Just shut up already," Ace finished my sentence for me and took hold of my waist, tossing me easily over his shoulder.

"Ace!" I screeched, struggling to free myself, already having been in this position once before. I didn't particularly want my butt on display for any people who were wandering outside the school. "Put me down!" I yelled, pounding my fists against his back.

He ignored me and continued walking as if he didn't even notice I was beating his back. I yelled at him again uselessly as he kept moving, pausing only once to readjust my position on his shoulder.

Oh no, not this again.

"Ace!" I yelled for the hundredth—no—millionth time.

"Shut up," he said, placing me on my feet when he finally stopped walking. Anger burned in my veins like fire and I put both my hands on his muscular chest, giving him a hard shove backwards, as if that would somehow make me feel better.

He grabbed my wrists at the same time he fell flat on his back and pulled me down with him, despite my efforts to escape his stony grip. Lying on the paved sidewalk, I breathed out and saw the sky, gray, gloomy and altogether unpleasant. It was a covered in fluffy dark clouds and snowflakes started to fall.

I shivered as I sat up, missing my jacket, forgetting that Ace was beside me. "I hate winter!" I screamed angrily, my emotions momentarily taking hold of my mind. It felt like everything was running on high and I couldn't stop it, no matter how hard I tried.

Everything that I tried to push away—my mom, my dad, everything—came back to me in a spontaneous rush and I choked on tears, trying my hardest not to cry. I was cold and angry, and that was not a very good combination for someone like me. "Hey," Ace said gently, offering me his hand. He'd already stood up and was waiting patiently with a look of concern etched onto his face.

I furiously wiped a tear that had escaped my eyes and stood up on my own, brushing past him. He was part of the reason behind why I was here right now and why I was so upset. It was his fault and I wasn't going to hesitate when it came to blaming him.

"Nova," he said, grabbing my arm.

"What?" I demanded, turning to look at him.

His eyes softened as he looked at me and he shrugged off his black jacket, draping it over my shoulders. I stood there speechless, not quite sure what to say.

"You don't have to hide what you're feeling from me," he murmured, inching closer to me. He cupped my cheek in his hand and used his thumb to brush a tear off my cheek.

"Yes, I do," I replied, pulling away from him.

"Why?" he asked, puzzled.

"I don't trust you, Ace," I breathed uncertainly and he scowled a little, but quickly wiped the look off his face.

I looked away, at the ground, and waited for him to say something.

"Nova," he muttered, tilting my chin back up. Before I could register what was happening, his warm lips were pressed against mine and I shivered—not because of the cold this time.

He pushed his mouth to mine and kissed me, slower and more passionately then he had at the library. I gave up resisting and kissed him back, my hand finding its way into his hair where my fingers curled around the short black tendrils.

He pulled back a little and I let go of his hair, mortified that I'd actually done that. He placed his hand on the back of my head and brought his lips to my forehead. He pressed them against my skin that burned under his touch and then backed up to look at me.

A smile tugged at the corners of his lips and I looked away to hide my own tiny grin. I pulled his jacket around me tighter as chills crept up my back. I really shouldn't be outside in this weather without proper clothing.

Neither of us said anything for a while. We just stood there absorbing what had just happened. "Are you cold?" Ace's gravelly voice broke the silence.

"Me? What about you?" I said, looking up at him. He was the one wearing a simple white t-shirt and dark jeans because he'd given me his jacket.

"I'm fine," he shrugged, crossing his arms over his chest. "You're cold," he observed when I didn't tell him the truth.

"I'm not," I protested and he rolled his eyes.

"Come on," he said, grabbing my hand. His flesh felt hot against mine as he pulled me by my hand behind him.

"Where are we going?" I asked, forcing my teeth not to chatter.

"Somewhere warm," he answered and I sighed, following him—although it wasn't actually my choice, given that his hand was glued to mine, his fingers gripping mine tightly.

"We could go back to school," I suggested, looking at the ground, but Ace shook his head no firmly. "Why is that?" I piped up curiously, referring to the fact that he'd left the school in such a hurry.

He pursed his lips and turned to look at me, his black

eyes searching mine. "I need you to do me a favor," he said, watching for my reaction.

"What do you mean?" I asked curiously and his eyes narrowed before he glanced down at his feet.

"Never mind, forget it," he said and although I was dying to know what he'd wanted, I didn't push him.

Something about the way he'd looked at me and then at the ground told me to leave it alone, and that was exactly what I was going to do.

He started walking again and I made my legs move, despite the numbness that was spreading through them. I was starting to regret following Ace and Shawn out of the school.

I absolutely hated the winter weather.

"Better?" Ace asked as I held a warm cup of hot cocoa from the local cafe in my hands. I moaned a yes as I took a delicious sip of the warm drink which made Ace chuckle in contentment. "Good," he said, leaning back against his side of the booth we were seated at.

The door chimed as someone walked in behind me and chills washed over me. I jumped in surprise at the sudden feeling. "Ace," a familiar voice acknowledged and we both turned to look up at whoever was speaking. The first thing I noticed about him was his spiky brown hair, sticking up in odd places. His hands were shoved into the pockets of his stylish jacket and I looked back over at Ace, realizing that Ace hadn't looked at him yet.

"Darrius," Ace answered coldly, his eyes were locked with mine, his beautiful blue orbs were holding my attention captive.

"Hi, Darrius," I said politely, tearing my stare away from

Ace. Darrius nodded in response and turned his head to look at me.

"Mind if I sit down?" he asked and I shook my head no, scooting over to make room for Darrius, when Ace jumped to his feet.

"Leave," he hissed at Darrius who rolled his eyes.

"You heard the lady. I can sit here," Darrius said gesturing to me with a wave of his hand. Ace's gaze hardened and he sat down beside me, instead of letting Darrius sit there.

Darrius sat down across from me and Ace, giving Ace a tired look, and studied us carefully. "So you two are a thing?" he asked, his voice deep and strained, as he twirled a twenty dollar bill around his long, dark slender fingers.

Ace and I looked at each other and spit out different answers, mine being a "no" and his being a "yes". He grabbed my hand under the table and I glanced over at him in surprise, our eyes locking together. "As soon as Darrius leaves, you're going to forget everything we say," Ace said quickly, the words spilling out of his mouth before I could look away, and my mind blanked as I nodded slowly.

My head felt heavy, like I wasn't in control of what was happening, and I turned to watch Ace and Darrius's conversation. "Really, Ace? You're going to pull that trick," Darrius said, rolling his eyes.

"Whatever Darrius, it works." Ace clenched his jaw and crossed his arms over his chest in an annoyed manner. "What do you want? Why are you here?" Ace asked rudely and if my head didn't feel so funny I probably would have chided his ill-manners.

Darrius gestured to me and shook his head. "Her. You know that."

"What's your problem, Darrius? Can't you leave it alone? Let me have this," Ace said, his voice hard and pleading at the same time. It probably should have surprised me that Darrius had said he'd wanted me and Ace was holding onto me like I was his lifeline, but it didn't. Nothing was registering in my head.

"Listen, Seth," Darrius started, Ace's body tensing at the foreign sounding name. "How can you ask that of me? You know what? You were never cut out to be an angel, that's why you fell–," Darrius started, sneering angrily, but Ace was by his side in an instant, his hands curling around Darrius's throat lifting him to his feet.

"Shut the hell up," Ace said, his words coming out clipped and threatening, and his lips curled up so menacingly.

"Seth-" Darrius choked out as Ace's hand tightened around his neck.

Ace let go of him with a simple "leave" and he watched as Darrius walked out of the cafe doors, shaking his head back and forth angrily. As soon as he walked out the door, when his foot crossed the threshold, I snapped back into reality, everything that had just happened already fading away from me. I tried uselessly to grasp onto a memory of what I'd just witnessed but it disappeared, and there I was sitting with Ace in the peaceful cafe, sipping hot cocoa.

Ace huffed in annoyance, running a hand through his hair. "Are you okay?" I asked and he looked up at me, as if he was startled by the sound of my voice.

"Fine," he said, wiping his angered expression off his face.

"How's the hot cocoa?" Ace teased, a grin reaching his lips. He smiled at me but it didn't reach his eyes, like the first time I'd gotten a good look at him, and I watched him curiously.

"It's good, thanks," I said, taking another sip as if to prove my point.

Ace looked satisfied by my answer and blew out a sigh, reaching across the table for my hand. I let him hold it and watched as he closed his eyes, breathing in and then out deeply. Ace used his thumb to rub gentle, soothing circles on the back of my hand and I felt instantly relaxed, happy to be here with him.

He brought my small hand to his lips and pressed a soft kiss on it where he'd traced the circles. I watched him, completely captivated, as he put my hand back down on the table. It felt cold at the absence of his touch and I longed to reach out and grab his hand again.

"Are you hungry?" Ace asked, pulling me from my thoughts.

"A little, but I can eat when I get home," I answered and he shook his head in response.

"I'll get you something," he said, jumping up to stand in the small line that had formed around the cashier. I watched as he went and stood with the small group of people, his back facing me. I sighed, wondering why he was so eager to get me some food.

I shook my head at his ridiculousness and sipped my drink, looking out the window at the light, fluffy snowflakes covering every inch of the ground.

# Chapter Seven

I tossed and turned, a sheen layer of sweat covering my entire body, making my bed sheets stick to my legs. Black eyes danced across my vision and I screamed, sitting bolt upright in bed, breathing heavily. My eyes searched the corners of the room frantically, terror coursing through me.

Someone was here, I was certain that someone was in my home. I snatched my phone off my bedside table and turned it on, squinting as the screen illuminated. It was 2:56 in the morning, way too early for me to be up on a Monday.

My attention perked as I heard a quiet thud, that sounded loud to my ears, and it made my heart pound in my chest. I fumbled with my phone as I dialed Ace's number. He'd taken my phone once and had programmed it in despite my futile protests. I held it up to my ear, praying that he would answer.

I pulled my blankets around me as if they'd somehow protect me from whatever was lurking outside my bedroom and let out a breath of relief when Ace picked up on the second ring. "Nova?" he answered. He sounded wide awake even though it was so early in the morning, but I didn't question it.

"Ace, where are you?" I breathed, trying my hardest to be quiet. I squeezed my eyes shut tightly, praying that for some reason he wasn't at his house, that he was somewhere close to mine.

"Doesn't matter, what's wrong?" he asked, brushing off my question.

"I think someone is in my house–," I whispered into the phone, listening to the sound of my hammering heart.

"I'll be there in ten minutes," he said and the line went dead. I dropped the phone beside me and wrapped my blanket around myself, my eyes refusing to open. I wasn't sure if I was imagining the sounds I was hearing or if they were really coming from outside my bedroom door. I suppressed a scared whimper and sat there, desperately wishing Ace would hurry up.

I don't know how long I waited but my breath caught in my throat when I heard loud, hollow footsteps. I quickly grabbed my hairbrush that was sitting on my nightstand beside my bed, holding onto the side that had the bristles. I clutched it tightly, preparing myself to use it as a weapon if needed. I watched in horror as the door handle twisted and tried to slow my breathing and calm the shaking in my hands.

Ace appeared in the doorway and I instantly relaxed, relieved that he was here. He walked over to where I was sitting, huddled in a cocoon of blankets, and he cupped my face in his hands. "I got you," he murmured, pulling me into a hug.

I threw my arms around him in relief, letting the brush fall to the floor with a thud, hugging him back tightly. He breathed in deeply, his chest rising as he did, and kept his arms around me.

After a while, he pulled back somewhat awkwardly and gave me a once over. I watched his Adam's apple bob in his throat as he swallowed. "What happened?" he asked and I pushed my hair out of my face, looking down.

"I don't know– I woke up and I heard something–," I said and he nodded sympathetically.

"I don't think anyone was here," he said, poking his head out of the room to sweep his eyes over everything one more time.

"Oh, okay. I'm sorry I called for no reason. I don't know what I was thinking," I said, letting out a frenzied laugh, starting to ramble.

"Hey, stop," he said gently, taking my face in his hands.

He pressed a kiss to my forehead and I melted under his touch, like butter on a warm piece of toast. "You can call me whenever," he said softly, and I smiled up at him gratefully. "You good now?" he asked, changing the subject smoothly, and I nodded.

"Thank you for coming," I said and he smiled.

"Anytime," he said, turning to leave.

I had to stop myself from reaching out and asking him to stay. I walked him to the door and I forced the growing pit of fear down, until I practically couldn't feel it. "See you later at school," he said, closing the door behind him. I quickly twisted the deadbolt into place and locked the handle as well, not taking any chances.

I turned around and leaned my back against the hard, cold wooden door and glanced treacherously around the room. I was too frightened to go back to sleep. I knew that, but I refused to call Ace and ask him to come back. He had other, more important things to do at three in the morning. It did strike me as odd that he had been out and about, but I wasn't going to judge him just yet.

I settled down on the couch, curling under a soft, wool blanket and I sat there until it was a normal time to wake up, until the sunlight leaked through the windows, giving the room a soothing yellow glow.

That's better, I thought. That's so much better.

I sniffled. My nose was stuffed and my eyes were red and watery. It was clear that I was sick. I debated on whether I should go to school or not but in the end, the rational part of my brain eventually won over. I barely had enough energy to stand up, let alone go to school. I guiltily looked at my phone, not wanting to have to tell Joe that I wouldn't be able to work my shift tonight. I knew he wouldn't be mad, but he would stress and be quietly disappointed. Maybe if I was feeling better I would be able to work.

I supposed that was what I got for staying up all night. I laid down in my bed, welcoming the soft, comforting mattress, and closed my eyes, breathing through my mouth. I had this sudden urge to call Ace and let him know I would be staying home, but I didn't because it didn't really concern him. He'd manage just fine without me.

In fact, it would most likely be me who needed him.

He'd become someone I was used to having around, someone who's presence was comforting to me. And that was a little scary. I hadn't let anyone in since my dad died. No one really, not even my aunt. And now there was this guy, who was crazy handsome, who'd slid into my life so easily and naturally. I sighed and snuggled deeper into my bed, the sweatpants and hoodie I'd slipped on keeping me comfortably warm.

I was so relaxed and sleepy that the knock that sounded at my door actually annoyed me, and I groaned but got up to answer it. I padded my way over to the front door and unlocked it, throwing it open, wiping my nose on my sleeve. I knew it was gross but I could wash my sweater later. I was too sick to care.

"Hey there, gorgeous," he said, smiling crookedly. It was so like him to show up right when I was thinking about him. I rolled my eyes and studied Ace as he stood outside my door.

"What are you doing here?" I asked and he smiled a little.

"You're sick, I'm here to help," he said, holding up a box of chicken noodle soup that he'd bought. I didn't even ask how he knew I was sick. I eyed the soup and then gave him a once over, trying to figure what strings would be attached to this.

"Are you cooking?" I asked, letting that be the final factor in my decision.

"Of course," he said and I sighed, my shoulders drooping slightly, and opened the door wider to let him in. He grinned and sauntered into the kitchen, and I instantly heard him rummaging through the cupboards and fridge.

"I was thinking we could go to the library later," he said around a mouthful of apple that he'd taken off the counter.

"Sure," I shrugged, not really caring.

"After you nap and eat soup, obviously," Ace added and I laughed.

"Okay, mom," I joked and he chuckled with me, filling a pot up with water. "I might have to work later, though," I added.

"And contaminate all the poor people's food? I don't think so," he said and I shook my head, chuckling to myself.

"Remember my friend Charles?" Ace asked, opening a package of the instant chicken noodle soup and dumping it into the pot of boiling water. I nodded and he continued. "He's going to meet us at the library," Ace said and I groaned inwardly because if there was one thing I hated, it was meeting new people. First impressions were always so hard for me, always, and there were never any exceptions.

"Sure," I said, rubbing my forehead that was warm, almost hot.

"You look beautiful," Ace said suddenly and I cracked a smile, leaning against the counter.

"I feel beautiful," I smiled sarcastically. He laughed and kissed my head, turning back to the soup leaving me with endless time to study the back of his head and ponder over what I'd gotten myself into by letting Ace into my life. A nagging feeling at the back of my mind told me that it couldn't possibly be good.

After I'd eaten and taken a shower, deciding that I didn't need that nap—even if it did sound pretty appealing—I was finally ready to go. "Women take so long to get ready," Ace, who had patiently waited on the couch, said and I shoved him lightly.

"It's a complicated process," I explained, not feeling apologetic about making him wait.

After all, he did proceed to return the favor twenty minutes later when we'd arrived at the library. I was wearing black skinny jeans, a dark olive green crop top with long sleeves and my hair was in a short, cute ponytail. I looked pretty good, considering I was sick. My jacket was folded over my arm and my feet were beginning to overheat in the boots I was wearing. I should have brought my shoes to change into, but I'd forgotten them at Joe's after my last shift.

The front of the library was buzzing with people, which demolished the "quiet" stereotype of a library because it sounded insanely loud in here. I was standing by a bookshelf, at the back of the library where there were less people, waiting for Ace who'd said he'd just be a minute. It had been two and I was impatiently thumping my foot on the ground with my arms crossed over my chest.

"Hey, beautiful," someone said, grinning at me.

"Hey," I greeted back warily, studying him. His hair was sandy blond and he had sharp piercing green eyes. They were as green as Ace's were dark blue, and I noticed that when he smiled, he had dimples, giving him a boyish look. His voice sounded oddly familiar yet I was sure I had never seen him before. I would have definitely recognized a face like that.

"What do you say about getting out of here?" he asked and I raised my eyebrows.

"A little forward don't you think?" I stalled, looking around for Ace. What was taking him so long? My eyes focused back on the stranger as he took my hand, tracing my fingers with his, stepping closer. My eyes widened and I attempted a sentence.

"Um, I'm here with, uh–" I sputtered, trying to explain that I was here with Ace. The blond guy leaned in close, brushing his lips against mine and I stood there, frozen in shock, and then I let out a loud, odd sounding laugh. Did that move really work on girls?

"Charles," I heard Ace bark, loud and short. The guy who had almost kissed me pulled away and turned to face Ace, whose angry face was staring at the stranger. I mean I would be too if I'd seen some random bimbo kissing Ace.

Not that we were dating–because we weren't. He was someone who was important to me who I occasionally made out with–yeah, definitely not dating. I'm sure Ace felt the same way too.

The stranger, Charles, backed up, his mouth agape. "This is your girl?" Charles said incredulously, still slowly moving back. I stopped myself from protesting against the "your girl" Charles had said, insinuating the very fact that I was trying so hard to deny. Ace launched himself at Charles and they both went tumbling to the floor in a heap of thrashing limbs and angry shouts.

"Ace!" I called, trying to grab him.

"I didn't know it was her!" Charles protested, trying to shove Ace off him.

"Ace stop!" I yelled and he did, getting off of Charles and

wiping his face. Charles rose into a standing position and Ace sneered at him, the air thick with tension.

Nobody said anything for a while until Ace pulled me protectively against him. I tried unsuccessfully to untangle myself from him, awkwardly pushing at his chest as he and Charles locked eyes, having a silent conversation.

"I'm sorry for kissing you," Charles apologized, scratching the back of his head after receiving a steely cold glare from Ace.

"It's okay, and by the way, that was a really lame pickup line," I said, relieved that they had stopped fighting before someone had actually gotten hurt.

"No, it's not okay," Ace snapped, glaring at his friend. Charles shrugged his shoulders, considering what I'd said.

"Hey, it's fine," I said, putting my hand on Ace's cheek and turning his head towards me. "It's fine," I repeated, reassuring Ace whose gaze had softened as he looked at me. I hadn't meant much by the statement. I was simply trying to calm him down because I could practically feel him vibrating with anger.

To my surprise, he nodded and sighed. Charles snorted from where he was and I glanced over at him. Ace looked up at him, angry again. "What now?" Ace sighed.

"Sorry, I just never took you to be the cuddly romance type," Charles laughed.

"I am not the 'cuddly romance type'," Ace objected, mocking Charles.

"Yes, you really are," Charles said, stifling laughter.

"No, I am not," Ace said, each word coming out clipped.

"Allow me," Charles said and Ace stepped back, holding his hands up daringly.

"November, is it?" Charles asked, grabbing my arm and gently pulling me over to him. I nodded in response to his question, watching what he was about to do curiously.

I had a sinking feeling that this was only going to make Ace angrier, and boy was I right.

"This is what you look like, Ace," Charles said, covering his face with his hands. When he removed them, his facial features had taken on a serious, brooding look.

"Don't touch her, Charles. She's mine," Charles cooed, mocking Ace who watched unimpressed as Charles took my hands in his.

"Don't worry about Charles. He's just a devilishly handsome, mysterious man," Charles said and Ace snorted at that one. I almost did too. Before I could've protested, Charles grabbed me and kissed me.

"Charles," Ace snarled, his eyes darkening, if that were possible. Charles pulled away, flashed Ace a grin and took off running through the rows of bookshelves. I wiped my mouth in disgust on the back of my sleeve and watched as Ace, who was completely livid, took off after him in full tilt.

"Guys! Be quiet, this is a library!" I whisper yelled as I began to chase them, having to stop, a cough wracking my small body.

# Chapter Eight

I chewed on my thumbnail out of boredom, randomly flipping through the pages of a National Geographic book. Staring at the rows upon rows of words, I gave a weary sigh. I glanced out of the corner of my eye, checking to see if Charles or Ace were as bored as me.

Charles was, that was for sure; but Ace was thoroughly engrossed in his phone, doing what looked like furiously texting someone. I wondered briefly who it was but then turned my focus back to the blonde. He was sitting upside down in his chair, his feet hanging off the top and his head brushing the floor. I scooted the tiniest bit closer and when neither Ace nor Charles noticed, I did it again.

I reached out and poked his taut stomach when I was within touching distance. He yelped and jumped up, his forehead narrowly missing the table. I grinned smugly at him, turning back to the book. "On no you don't," he said into my ear, taking the book from my hands.

"I was reading that," I remarked dryly, trying to grab it from where he was dangling it over my head.

As soon as I stretched my arm up, his fingertips brushed over my exposed stomach and I screamed, throwing my hand over my mouth to muffle the noise. "Shh," Charles nagged, repeating what I'd yelled at them earlier. "We're in a library."

I shook my head in disbelief and glared at him, lunging for his stomach and tickling his sides. He writhed under my touch and let out a strained, clipped laugh. He grabbed my wrists which stopped me from tickling him and I sighed, sitting back down in my chair.

"Now that you're done feeling up his abs," Ace said gruffly in my ear making me jump. I tried to protest because I was most definitely not 'feeling up his abs' but Ace kept talking. "I was thinking we could go for dinner."

"Sweet!" Charles exclaimed, smiling widely. "I'm starving," he added pointedly, lifting up his shirt to rub his stomach— or, in my opinion, reveal his very hard six pack.

Ace rolled his eyes because obviously he hadn't been talking to Charles about dinner, but I didn't have the heart to tell him. "He can come," I said quietly in Ace's ear. Ace sighed and took my hand, helping me to my feet even though I was quite capable of standing on my own.

Charles stood up, smacking the table as he did, knocking all our books off onto the floor. "Wonderful," Ace muttered.

"You are so dumb," I told Charles, but I couldn't stop the smile that spread across my entire face.

"Am not," he protested, helplessly looking at the mess he'd made.

"Are too," I argued.

"No."

"Yes."

"No."

"No," I said, grinning smugly, knowing that I had him.

"Yes," he answered.

"Ha," I said, feeling pleased with myself, and stuck my tongue out at him.

"Whatever," he said, fake pouting before an involuntary smile lit up his face and I poked his cheek.

He stopped smiling, his dimples disappearing along with his smile and he stared at me puzzled. "What was that for?" he asked, frowning slightly.

"What was what for?" I asked, feigning innocence.

"You were making fun of my dimples."

I covered my mouth with my hand, smothering my laughter. "You were!" he exclaimed, completely outraged.

"Sorry," I giggled unapologetically.

"My mom told me they were charming and cute," he said and I couldn't help but laugh at his ridiculousness. "Wouldn't you agree?" he asked.

"Sure Charles," I said skeptically and he grinned. "You're an idiot," I told him as I shook my head.

"Am not."

Here we go again.

"Are too."

"Are you two five?" Ace asked, butting into the conversation as he stood up with a pile of books in his hands.

"What can I say, Nova? You bring out the child in me," Charles said. I placed a hand over my heart and gave a small gasp.

"I'm flattered."

Ace rolled his eyes and grit his teeth together in annoyance, and Charles pulled me into a hug. His scent was nothing compared to Ace's. Charles smelt of ivory soap and fresh mint. I inhaled deeply, smiling into his chest, before I pushed him away. I bent down to help Ace, who was glaring at Charles. I began to clean up inside, and sighed, looking at the National Geographic book that was open on the floor.

Did you know that a shrimp's heart is in its head?

All three of us, Ace, Charles and I, made our way out to

Ace's car, the black Dodge Charger in the library parking lot, and piled inside. Charles was the unlucky one who got to sit in the backseat, but that was a given because he was kind of the third wheel and I'd only let him come because I'd felt bad about leaving him out.

"So where are we going?" Charles asked, leaning forward to stick his head between our seats.

"You'll see," Ace muttered, annoyed with Charles for tagging along. I blew out a sigh as Charles turned his head to look at me.

"Do you know where we are going?" he questioned, clearly disliking surprises as much as I did.

"I don't," I said.

When we arrived at the restaurant, Ace looked a little dejected as he walked up to order our food. My eyes followed him and I bit my lip, not sure what to do. "So what's the deal with you and him?" Charles asked, bringing my attention to him.

"Me and who?" I said.

"You and Ace," he laughed. The deal with me and Ace? He hadn't even officially asked me to be his girlfriend yet, so as far as I was concerned, Ace was just a friend, maybe a little bit more than that.

"Oh," I started, studying the scratched light colored wood of the table we were seated at. "Nothing," I shrugged and Charles laughed.

"I'm serious."

"So am I," I answered, looking up to meet his gaze. "We're not dating–even though he acts like it sometimes–we're just friends, nothing more," I sighed and rested my chin on my hand, taking a nice long look at Ace.

"Yeah, okay. 'Friends', I feel you," Charles said, winking, and I shook my head no.

"Just friends, Charles," I said. He obviously didn't believe me but he didn't push any further, just changed the subject to something less serious.

"Here," Ace said, sitting down beside me and kissing the side of my head. My eyes locked with Charles's who raised an eyebrow inquisitively. I scooted away from Ace after politely thanking him for the food. I wanted to show Charles I meant what I said, that Ace and I weren't dating.

I could feel Ace's gaze burn holes into the side of my head but I didn't look over. I did squirm uncomfortably in my seat though. I stared hard at my food, memorizing the small, intricate pattern on the plate and I traced it with the tip of my fork. Charles excused himself to use the washroom and I acknowledged him with a nod of my head, swallowing the thick lump in my throat.

I felt Ace's hand on mine and I turned towards him, to see him watching me worriedly. "What's wrong?" he asked and I debated with myself if I should just blurt out the truth or tell a lie. I opted for the latter.

"I'm just not feeling well," I said, shrugging.

"Nova," he groaned, "tell me the truth." I sighed, looking up at him.

"We're not dating," I said and he looked a little taken aback at my sudden statement. I could sort of tell he was upset or angry, one or the other, but I was simply letting him know in case he'd been confused.

"I know, but I thought we were close to that–" he said, uncertainty lingering in his voice. I studied him for a moment, debating on what to say, but I sighed and shook my head.

"Ace, I–," I started, looking away. "I don't trust you," I muttered and he gaped at me in disbelief. "I mean, yeah, I care about you and I appreciate all the things you do for me, but anyone could go out to the store and buy a box of soup or show up at my door when I have a nightmare.

You've never done anything that proves I can trust you," I said truthfully, letting the words pour out of me.

"What can I do?" he asked and I looked at him with confusion. "What can I do to prove you can trust me?" he asked, rephrasing his question.

"I don't know," I answered, shrugging. "I guess it just takes time," I murmured and he pursed his lips, sitting back in his chair.

"Okay, that's fine," he said gently although his tense body didn't seem like 'it was fine'.

Charles walked back over to the table stopping to lean down and discreetly whisper something in Ace's ear. I didn't hear exactly what he said but it sounded something like "if only you were actually worth trusting." I shook my head because now I was just imagining things. Charles hadn't heard our conversation therefore he hadn't said that to Ace.

He'd whispered something else and my crazy imagination had come up with what I'd thought I'd heard.

"How's the food, November?" Charles asked, an effortless smile tugging at his lips.

"Great," I smiled, although I wasn't really enjoying this meal. The food was fine but the air felt thick with tension. Ace seemed mad but he said he wasn't. And that was exactly why I couldn't trust him. He kept secrets from me. He was always doing something else when he was with me. I wasn't asking him to tell me every single thing about himself, but I didn't like the secrecy.

My head was starting to pound and I dropped my fork on my plate loudly. It clattered against the glass and both boys looked up, startled almost. I rubbed my temples soothingly, but the aching in my skull refused to subside. I groaned and I felt Ace's arm around my shoulders, pulling me against his chest. He murmured something in my ear that sounded an awful lot like 'sleep' in Spanish or Italian, one of those impossible to understand languages. My eyes grew heavy and my mind drifted off, leaving Ace with me sleeping against him, exactly like he'd wanted.

"Really, Ace? I liked hanging out with her," Charles pouted, I could still hear him say as I drifted off to sleep.

"Some other time, Charles," Ace said, pressing his lips to my head. Not that I could actually feel it. I was sleeping soundly, oblivious to anything and everything that was going on around me. They continued talking though, but I guess it wasn't my place to hear their private conversation.

"I'm holding you to that," Charles said and Ace grumbled something. "I wish it didn't have to be her," Charles sighed.

"But it does, Charles. Don't get all soft now that you've met her. You know what we need to do," Ace said and Charles nodded, looking away from my sleeping body.

If they were going to talk about me behind my back, I would definitely have to try and stay awake next time.

Next time, the thought drifted around in my otherwise empty mind.

My head lolled to the side and I jerked upright, my eyes wrenching open. I waited a moment for my vision to adjust to wherever I was, and I looked around. I was in my house, on the couch. Charles was there, bent over the table focusing hard on something. "Charles?" I asked and he jumped, dropping whatever was in his hand.

"Oh, you're awake," he said, glancing nervously between me and what he'd dropped. I squinted and then rolled my eyes, bringing my gaze back to Charles.

"You broke the table," I said, thoroughly unamused and he smiled sheepishly, scratching the back of his head.

"It was an accident," he offered and I rubbed my forehead tiredly.

"Where's Ace?" I asked, yawning.

"He went out and he asked me to watch you," Charles answered, tossing the piece of broken table away. I frowned because I wasn't a baby, I didn't need to be watched.

I looked at the unassuming boy in my living room and an idea sparked in my brain. I was going to pry Charles for answers. "How long have you and Ace known each other?" I asked nonchalantly, trying to make it sound like I wasn't interested, but my eyes were locked on him.

"Oh you know, a couple thousand, uh, days. Ever since we were little," he squeaked the last part out, and I nodded. That seemed normal enough, except for his choice of time measurement. A couple thousand days? But, Charles was weird like that.

"Where did you grow up?" I asked and he frowned.

"Oh for God's sake, I can't remember what the town is called," he mumbled under his breath and I let out a loud laugh.

"Of course you would forget where you grew up," I said, shaking with laughter. He smiled, his dimples appearing on his face, and his cheeks flushed red. He ran a hand through his golden locks and stared at me.

"Is there something on my face?" I asked, frowning.

"Just a little bit of drool…" he trailed off and I gasped, reaching up to touch my face.

"There is not!" I said, launching myself off the couch and making my way quickly, running basically, to my bathroom.

"You liar," I called to him, walking back out to where he was laughing on the ground.

"You believed me," he said innocently.

"How did you break my table?" I shot at him unexpectedly, raising an eyebrow at him. His smile slowly faded and he stared at me, his face a mixture of embarrassment and disbelief.

"That doesn't matter. What matters is that you haven't eaten in a few hours. Are you hungry? I can cook–yeah, I'm a really great cook," he mumbled, heading for the kitchen. I giggled and followed him, trying not to burst into hysterical laughter.

"It's not funny," he muttered as he raided the fridge, looking for any good food. Cooking was an art, of sorts. It took skill and precision, like dancing or drawing. Charles looked like he might actually be a good cook, judging by the way he'd grabbed everything he needed so quickly.

Or maybe he'd just grabbed the first things he'd laid eyes on–but I wasn't going to judge until after I'd tasted whatever he was making.

I regretted thinking that as I stared down at the brown blob of–I didn't even know what–and I looked up at Charles' eager and hopeful face.

"Voilà!" he'd exclaimed as he'd put the plate down in front of me, letting me gulp in horror at the thought of eating what he'd concocted. I guess the fact that I had a heart was why I was lifting the spoon full of the brown goo to my mouth, praying to any God out there that this wouldn't kill me.

"What are you trying to feed my girl?" Ace asked as he barged into the house without knocking, might I add, rather loudly, causing me to drop the spoon back into the bowl. It slowly sunk down into the glob of what resembled chocolate pudding until it was completely covered.

"I'm not your girl," I muttered and Ace sighed, rolling his eyes at me in annoyance.

"I just saved you from having to eat... that. You should be at least a little grateful," Ace said, pointing to my bowl and I nodded in agreement.

"You're right. I am grateful," I smiled sweetly as I stood up.

"Where are you going?" Ace asked, following me down the hall.

"I'm going to get a sweater. I'm cold," I answered and he stopped me, grabbing my arm.

"Take mine," he murmured, easily slipping his hoodie over his head.

"My closet is literally two feet away," I replied dismissively, eyeing the sweater skeptically.

"I'm aware of that, captain obvious, but you look nice in my clothes," he breathed, his frustration with me evident in his voice. I studied his face. His sharp jawline, high cheekbones, and long lashes all contributed to his overall good looks. At that moment, I realized any girl would kill to be in my position right now. Any girl, but me.

I sighed and took the sweater from him, slipping it over my head. He smiled goofily as I fixed my hair, taking it out of the ponytail and putting it back in. "There," he said, taking a step back to look at me as if he were an artist admiring his latest masterpiece. The way he looked at me, with such intensity, made my cheeks tinge red and I felt heat creeping up my neck. If he didn't stop watching me like that, I was going to have to take the sweater back off.

I brushed past him and returned to the kitchen where Charles was eating my plate for me. Alarmed, I hurried over to where he was and snatched the almost empty plate away. "Are you crazy?" I hissed, taking the fork from his hand.

"Jeez, sorry. There's more in the pot for you," he grumbled and I lightly placed the dishes on the counter, standing in front of Charles.

I pushed my hand against his forehead and he watched me curiously, his eyes darkening the tiniest bit. "What are you doing?" he growled and I jumped back at the sudden sharpness in his voice. I squared my shoulders defensively and glared at him. "I was making sure you didn't have a fever from eating that gross crap," I said and his features softened just a touch.

"Oh," he said, his shoulders relaxing. I leaned against the counter, crossing my arms and I stared at the ground. Something about the way Charles's mood changed so fast had me reeling, alarm bells ringing inside my head.

"You know, I'm not feeling well. I think it's best if you both leave and give me some, uh, time to rest," I lied, addressing Charles, and Ace who'd just walked in the room.

"I can stay if you want," Ace offered. Charles stayed quiet from his place at the table. I guessed he probably knew that it was his fault I'd asked them to leave.

"I'm probably at the infectious stage of the cold right now. No point in us all getting sick," I said, smiling and offering a measly cough as validation. In reality, I don't think either of the two boys would have gotten sick if they had stayed, but better safe than sorry. At least that was my excuse.

Ace didn't look too impressed, but let me escort them both to the door. Ace kissed my cheek adding, "Call me when you feel better," which made a guilty knot form in my stomach because I'd lied. Don't get me wrong. I didn't feel my best, definitely not one hundred percent, but it wasn't completely unbearable. I just hadn't wanted the guys to stay here any longer. That was reasonable, right?

"Yeah, of course," I smiled a little closing the door as soon as they'd walked out, not having said goodbye to Charles. His sudden anger before had scared me the slightest bit and I think he knew that, which was why he'd left in such a hurry.

I slid the deadbolt into place, urging my pounding heart to slow back to a normal pace and I sat down on the couch, pulling a woolen blanket around my shoulders. In a few minutes it would start to itch and I would be forced to get up and find a different blanket, but for now this one would do. In fact, if I fell asleep fast enough, I wouldn't even notice the uncomfortable scratchy feeling.

I closed my eyes briefly, reviewing everything that had happened today.

Ugh, I thought. School tomorrow.

Despite the fact that I'd told the boys I needed rest, it didn't stop Ace from showing up a couple hours later. He stood at my door, looking rather handsome with his disheveled, black hair and his stark white t-shirt. It was hard for me to focus on him at that moment. Heck it was hard for me to keep my eyes open.

"You're back," I mumbled, balling my hands into fists to rub my eyes. I'd just woken up from a long nap and I was still a bit disoriented, everything feeling like it was still part of a dream. He smiled gently down at me but he looked a little awkward, like he wasn't sure what to say or do. It was certainly not a look that suited Ace. He was usually the cocky, overconfident type. Not at all the shy, nice guy.

"Yeah, I'm just checking up on you," he said, his voice thick and unintentionally gruff.

"Come in," I yawned, my eyes watering as I opened the door wide enough so he could come through.

"Thanks," he said, shoving his hands into his pockets as he slipped off his shoes and made his way further into the house. "You just wake up?"

"Yeah," I answered, smiling at him. "Is it that obvious?" I asked sheepishly, pulling my hair into a low ponytail to hopefully hide the frizz that had no doubt appeared. "Nova," he said sternly, tilting my chin up. "You always look gorgeous."

"Thanks Ace," I said, studying the floor and trying my hardest not to let my cheeks turn red. It was a battle I quickly lost, and I sighed, meeting his intense gaze. He smirked a little at the sight of my flushed face and I rolled my eyes. It struck me as odd that we were so comfortable together that we could simply stand in the hallway for minutes just watching and observing one another silently.

"Are you hungry? Or tired? Do you need anything?" he asked all at once and I could easily tell that he was trying hard to prove that I could trust him.

"I'm just still a little sleepy," I admitted and he chuckled, grabbing my hand.

"Go back to sleep then," he suggested and I shrugged, sitting down beside him on the couch.

"I can't because you're here. Most people stay awake when they have guests over," I said in a 'duh' tone, laughing as he gave me a blank look.

"What if your guest is sleeping too?" he asked and I furrowed my brow, pondering his question.

"Lie down," he said, pulling me practically on top of him as he kicked his feet up onto the couch and he looked down at me, smiling. I narrowed my eyes but found that he was weirdly comfortable.

Maybe it was his strange scent of worn leather and cinnamon that made me feel at home, or possibly the fact that I did feel safer whenever Ace was around. As we laid on the couch together we both grew still, falling slowly asleep. I smiled to myself, gently snuggling closer to him.

If it wasn't for the slight rise and fall of his chest, I would have thought he was dead. His hands were cold to the touch yet searing hot at the same time and he was utterly still. His facial features looked angelic, I thought to myself, and then chuckled lightly at the absurd thought.

"What?" Ace asked, the corners of his mouth quirking up. I probably should have guessed that he wasn't sleeping.

"You look like an angel," I told him truthfully, not hiding what I was thinking because those were the worst kind of people, the ones who constantly hid from everything, and he smiled. "How would you know what an angel looked like?" he asked and I laughed.

He opened his eyes to look at me, the deep, endless blue of his irises piercing me, as they did every time we made eye contact. "I'm not an angel, Nova. I'm anything but," he said darkly and I smiled although I suppose I should have been a little worried by the tone his voice had taken.

"You're my angel," I said and he gently touched my cheek, an indescribable emotion glinting in his eye. I smiled and closed my eyes, remembering what it felt like to let someone into my life, to let someone care. And then reality settled back in, bursting my bubble of short lived happiness and brick by brick, I built my walls all the way back up to the top.

I pulled back a bit, sitting up, and closed my eyes briefly as I cursed myself for letting him get this close. I guess it was time to do what I'd always done and push him away, as far from my life as I could make him get, shutting him out and locking myself away.

But hadn't I just said that the people who hid from things, the people who couldn't face their problems head on, were the worst kind? So why was I resorting back to hiding? The answer to that question was simple for me. Why let people into your life when they would just be wrenched away?

"What's wrong?" Ace asked, carefully watching me, his expression becoming guarded.

"What? Nothing," I deflected, getting off the couch and flicking the kitchen light on.

"Wait, what just happened?" Ace asked, sounding confused and hurrying after me. He glided across the floor gracefully and silently, as if he wasn't even there. I shrugged in response to his question.

I felt his hand on my shoulder and he spun me around to face him. My eyes darted away from his, looking anywhere but at him. "Hey, November," Ace said loudly, his voice softening as he touched my face gently. "Don't," he started and I pulled away, watching him harshly.

"Don't what?"

"Don't shut me out," he said, sighing, and he raked his long, pale fingers through his hair. He shoved his hands into his pockets, a helpless look on his face as I took a step backwards, baffled by what he'd said. He gave another sigh and moved closer to me, inching his way forward. "You don't have to push me away," he said, his voice involuntarily thick with emotion.

"Yes, I do."

"Why?" he asked.

"Because," I shrugged, not really answering his question.

"Look, I get it. You lost someone you loved and now you're scared to let me in," he started tentatively and he watched me bristle with anger.

"How did you know that?" I said accusingly and crossed my arms over my chest. I was certain I'd never told Ace anything about my parents. In fact I'd barely told anyone who didn't need to know. His facial features hardened for a second and I smiled inwardly, feeling somewhat smug for being able to break through his act and make him angry. But he reigned in his anger and frustration at my stubbornness and wiped the look of his face.

"Please, November," he pleaded, noticeably ignoring my accusatory question, and folded his hands over mine. "I won't hurt you, I promise."

Something small inside me didn't believe him, wanted me to push him away from me, make him leave. But a bigger part of me yearned to trust him. I really did want to let him in and stop fighting. I hadn't realized that I wanted that until it hit me square in the face like a slap, a rather rude awakening to my feelings, and I had to catch myself before latching onto him.

He must have seen the indecisiveness in my eyes because he pulled me into a tight hug, holding my small frame against his chest and his arms encircled me, as if that would somehow convince me. I sighed, leaning into the touch.

Would it be that bad?

Yes, it really would.

No, it really wouldn't.

What do you know?

Nothing.

Exactly.

My mind babbled away, arguing and pleading with me.

I guess maybe I should have listened to the angry, pleading voice inside my head, but I didn't.

I brought my arms around his waist, returning his hug, and willed the motion to convey everything I was feeling, that I was going to let him in and trust him with all my heart, even if I was still a little uncertain.

"I'm here and I'm not going anywhere," he murmured and I knew that he understood. "I promise," he added softly, pressing his perfect lips to the top of my head and then he held me for what felt like forever. We stood there like that, in the doorway between the kitchen and the living room, holding onto each other tightly, not wanting to let go.

Ace's phone started buzzing and I pulled away to let him answer. He reluctantly took his phone from his pocket and held it up to his ear after swiping to answer the call. "Hello?"

"Oh hey," Ace said, leaning against the wall, glancing briefly at me. I wondered who he was talking to but eventually shrugged and sat down on the back of the couch so I could remain facing him. "Yeah, we're good to go," he told the person on the other end of the call. "Okay, bye Charles."

It was Charles. I grinned to myself, because Charles was happy and it was infectious, just thinking about him brought a smile to my mostly impassive face. "What'd he want?" I asked Ace who shook his head dismissively in response and I watched as he shoved his phone back to where he grabbed it from.

"I have to go," he said and I nodded, staring hard at the floor. It wasn't like we'd just had a heart to heart conversation about never leaving each other, no, nothing like that. I fought the urge to roll my eyes at my sarcasm and looked back up at Ace who was looking at me with an unreadable expression.

"I'll see you later, okay?" he assured me and I smiled a little, nodding my head.

"Bye," I said once he was out the door. I closed it and was starting to walk away when a knock sounded through the apartment. I threw it open, forgetting to look at who it was because I had assumed it was Ace.

"Did you forget something-" I started to say but then the guy smiled sheepishly at me and I abruptly stopped talking. "Darrius?"

"Hey, November," he said, scratching the back of his head.

"Hey..." I trailed off uncertainly, watching him closely. "What are you doing here?" I asked, my voice holding an accusatory hint.

"I need to tell you something, ah, screw this" he said, abandoning his first approach for one of utter rudeness, and I gaped at him as he shoved passed me, swinging the door shut behind him.

"You can't just come in here," I said, anger pooling in my stomach. I briefly thought about calling Ace and telling him to get his jerk of a friend out of my house, but I wasn't going to be that kind of girl, the kind who called their boyfriend whenever they needed something. I was a big girl, I could handle it on my own.

"Technically, I can, considering I bought you this place," he smirked and I raised my eyebrows, personally insulted by his statement. I had watched my aunt go to work every single day and stay at the office late every night to pay for these apartments.

"You really don't remember?" he said, checking his watch as if he had somewhere else to be and he was running late. "Okay, this will be easier," he said, not waiting for my response to his question, and started moving closer to me. I backed up instinctively and slapped at his hand as he reached for me.

"Please don't be like that, Aella," he said and I stared at him like he'd grown a second head. This guy was either high as a kite or completely mental. Either way, he needed to get out of my house.

"You really need to leave," I said, my voice betraying me and shaking the smallest bit.

"No, you need to remember. And don't worry. Dad already approved," he grinned before placing his palm flat on my forehead. I had intended to wrench myself out of his grip but as soon as his skin had come in contact with mine it was like my mind failed me.

I had no control whatsoever over my body and I felt myself growing drowsier, succumbing to Darrius's influence. My eyes slipped shut and I tumbled forward into his outstretched arms, his hand never lifting off my forehead.

# Chapter Nine

I woke up in my bed with a cold cloth stuck to my forehead. I let my eyes flutter open. Ace and Charles were sitting on either side of me. Charles was fiddling with something in his hands and Ace was worriedly staring at the floor. "Guys?" I rasped, my throat feeling way too dry.

"Nova," Ace said, his voice mixed with relief and another emotion I couldn't identify.

"What happened?" I asked, reaching for a glass of water that Ace promptly brought to my lips.

"That crazy dude attacked you," Charles said incredulously and my eyes widened.

"He attacked me?"

"Yeah, oh God I was so scared. I thought you were dead when we walked in. I swear, I wish I could find that guy and beat the crap out of him," Charles admitted and I half nodded, half chuckled. It was hard to take Charles seriously. He was too much of a goofy, aloof person to think he would ever be able to do something to harm someone.

Leave it to Charles to make me laugh when I feel like crap in every way possible. "I'm glad you're okay," Ace said gruffly and I turned my attention to him. His greeting had sounded so much less sincere than Charles' but Ace wasn't the kind of guy who poured his heart out all the time, and I knew that. His dark hair was disheveled and hanging around his face loosely. His jaw was set squarely and he was clenching his teeth.

"What's wrong?" I croaked, reaching for more water.

"Nothing," he said, a bit too curtly to be believable. Charles pulled my gaze back to him when he got up, searching intently through his phone.

"Here!" he exclaimed as he held his phone up triumphantly. "Found it," he grinned and I was about to ask what exactly it was he found when he started playing music.

It was random and completely out of the blue but Charles put on Justin Bieber, and to be precise, his song 'Baby'. I wrinkled my nose at the sound of the intro playing because it was such an old song and I could not even begin to fathom why Charles had it on his phone.

"Turn that off," Ace barked and Charles's smile drooped as he sighed and turned the music off. I, for one, was a little excited to see Charles sing 'Baby' by Justin Bieber, but clearly Ace didn't feel the same way. It was a shame that some people didn't appreciate the fine arts.

"I was just trying to cheer her up," Charles muttered but Ace ignored him, focusing on me.

"Do you remember anything about what happened?" Ace asked intently, his gaze burning holes into me.

"No," I said, racking my brain to try and think of anything, anything at all. Ace's shoulders visibly relaxed when I told him I couldn't remember what had happened and I stared at him, feeling puzzled.

"You should get some more rest," Ace suggested and I nodded, trying not to stare at him oddly.

"Yeah," I agreed, I really should.

It was weird. I could remember what happened right up until Ace left and then everything else was abruptly cut off.

It was like nothing had even happened and when I thought about it for too long or too hard, my head started to hurt, a steady throbbing in the back of my skull.

I groaned and rolled over to face the wall of a human that was lying beside me on the bed. Ace had left a while ago, leaving me alone with my thoughts and Charles. I'd tried to convince Charles to leave but he was very adamant that he had to stay to "watch over me" or something like that. I'd rolled my eyes at that, but let him stay nonetheless.

"You okay?" Charles asked, his bright green eyes opening to look at me.

"Yeah," I sighed, giving him a small, tentative smile. There was something, I didn't know what, but there was definitely something that the boys weren't telling me.

It was easier to tell with Charles even though I'd only met him a couple days ago, but he was visibly on edge and it was a little unnerving. It made me feel jittery and nervous and I felt the need to keep looking over my shoulder. A giant, looming elephant was hanging around in the room except I was the only one who didn't know what it was.

That's why I'd been relieved when Ace had left, because something about the idea of him keeping such a big secret from me–already, considering we had just become, well, whatever we were–was angering and annoying. God, there were just too many thoughts and emotions going through my head.

I watched as strands of sandy blond hair fell into Charles's eyes and he blinked, keeping his gaze locked with mine. "What's wrong?" he asked and I mentally face palmed. His knee nudged mine as I shrugged and lied, telling him everything was fine.

"You know, I'd tell you if something had happened earlier," he said softly and it was like someone had dumped a pail of ice water on my head, because he had known exactly what I was thinking. I quickly pulled my leg away from his and flipped over, burying my face in the pillow. What the heck was up with both of those boys, Ace and Charles? They both seemed to know exactly what I was thinking all the time.

"You hungry?" Charles asked, poking the side of my stomach with his finger and I squirmed away from his touch and gave him a disgusted look, remembering the weird blob he'd concocted for me last time I'd mentioned food.

"Definitely not," I laughed when he pouted.

"You don't like my cooking?" he said. I could tell by the way his dimples appeared on his face that he was joking.

I checked the time quickly, and then set an alarm that would wake me up in a few hours so I could go to school. I couldn't keep hanging around at home. It wasn't productive or good for my future. School was important and recently I'd been skipping out on my responsibilities and commitments. Plus, I had offered to work tonight and I was thinking about picking up an extra hour after my shift to make up for calling in sick yesterday.

I rolled my eyes and closed them, feeling incredibly tired considering I'd slept for a good amount of time. "Goodnight," I heard Charles say in my ear as he pulled the covers up to my chin, gently tucking me in. I mumbled a quick response and let myself fall asleep, succumbing to the everlasting tiredness.

"Wake up," I said, yawning as I shook Charles's shoulders back and forth. I'd managed to roll him onto his back so then I could at least see his face but he was still sleeping soundly, his mouth parted slightly as he breathed. "Charles," I whined, patting him on both cheeks which still did nothing. "I need to get going and I can't leave you here," I muttered to his sleeping figure which was so stubborn.

"Hello," I drawled, grabbing my glass of water off the nightstand. I then proceeded to dump it on his face and watched with satisfaction as he sat up quickly, his eyes wide.

"What happened?" he immediately asked and I chuckled. He pushed some of his sopping wet hair out of his eyes and he glared at me. "Was that necessary?"

"Yes! It really was, Charles. You wouldn't wake up," I said loudly and he laughed, swinging his feet off the side of the bed. His shirt crept up his back as he stretched lazily and I gasped, my mouth hanging open.

"So why are we getting up?" he was asking and when I didn't answer he turned to look at me.

"What is on your back?" I questioned in shock and his mouth formed the shape of an o while he cursed himself silently.

At the hem of his shirt where it had risen, I'd seen the tips of two jagged white scars in what looked to be an upside down V shape. "Scars," he answers slowly, as if he was picking his words carefully. "I got them a long time ago," he told me, turning around to face me completely. "They don't hurt anymore," he assured me after seeing my mortified expression, his eyes softening a bit.

"What's going on?" Ace asked, appearing at the door. I jumped and faced him, surprised because I hadn't even heard him come in.

"Nothing," Charles responded coolly, standing up and crossing his arms over his chest. He shot me a look that Ace didn't catch and I swallowed the lump in my throat, shaking my head to somewhat clear my thoughts.

Ace raised a suspicious eyebrow at me and I shrugged it off, blinking a few times. "Come on, Nova," Ace said after a moment, reaching for my hand. He pulled me into the hallway and grinned at me, cupping my face in his hands gently. "What do you say about going to dinner later?" Ace asked and I shook my head no, a small smile making its way onto my face.

"I have to work," I shrugged, kissing his cheek. "Rain check?" I asked and he nodded, sighing as he watched me.

"You're way too dedicated," he laughed a bit and I shrugged.

I let go of Ace's hand, heading back into my apartment to get ready for school. I couldn't neglect my studies for any longer, as much as I'd wanted to. I shooed Charles out of my room so I could get ready and once I was done, he stopped me as I walked out my bedroom door. "Don't tell Ace about the scars," he muttered through gritted teeth, his face more livid than any other time I'd seen it.

"I won't, I promise," I said quickly to calm his nerves and he nodded, breathing in deeply.

"Thanks," he said quickly before leaving.

"Bye," I muttered to myself, waving to where he disappeared. I grumbled something else under my breath and turned to go into my bathroom. "Holy crap!" I screamed, tilting my head up and breathing in through my nose to stop my heart from thudding so hard. It didn't feel normal in my chest, but that was probably a given seeing as how Ace had just scared the bejesus out of me. "Ace!" I exclaimed exasperatedly, shaking my head and continuing to take deep breaths.

"Sorry," he smiled sheepishly, clearly not actually sorry. I waved off his apology and leaned against the wall until I remembered what I was supposed to be doing.

"I have to brush my teeth," I informed Ace, trying to push past him to get into the washroom. Ace suddenly stopped and backed me up against the wall, his expression turning serious.

"Did Charles show you his scars?" he asked, narrowing his eyes at me as if he could see the answer by looking through me.

I battled with myself for a moment, contemplating if I should tell the truth or lie, keeping my promise to Charles, but something told me he already knew. Perhaps it was because he had been eavesdropping on our conversation from his sneaky hiding place. "Yes," I answered and he clenched his teeth, nodding his head.

"Of course he did," Ace sighed and I pulled my hand out of his grip, distancing myself from him the smallest bit.

"Did he say anything about mine?" Ace asked, pinching the bridge of his nose.

"You have scars too?" I asked, my mouth agape. He pursed his lips when he realized I hadn't known he had scars, that he'd just given himself away, but he nodded stiffly. The atmosphere felt too thick with tension and I closed my eyes briefly, wishing it would magically disappear, evaporate into the air.

I cleared my throat, a feeble attempt to change the conversation, and Ace took the hint, moving out of the way to grant me access to the bathroom. I grabbed my toothbrush, which was green like my eyes, and I smeared a blob of toothpaste onto the brush. It was a little unnerving to have Ace hovering over my shoulder as I brushed my teeth but I didn't want to upset him more than he already was.

"Let's get to school," he said once I'd finished and I nodded, taking a hold of his hand comfortingly. "Man, I can't wait for Spanish class," he sighed as we got into the car and I smiled at him.

"I hate Spanish class," I informed him and he laughed.

"I meant because I get to spend time with you," he told me.

"I know, I was just messing with you," I chuckled playfully and he pursed his lips as he started the car.

I looked out the window while he pulled out of the parking space, making a mental checklist of everything I had to accomplish today. It felt like I hadn't seen Joe in forever. Jen and Shawn too. I furrowed my brow as I thought about what had happened the other day with Shawn, but shook my head, warding off any negative thoughts. Shawn worked there full-time whereas I was only a part time employee, therefore we were always there at the same time so I guess I would see how he acted when I got to the diner later tonight for my shift.

"Good to see you, Clumsy!" Joe exclaimed cheerfully as I walked through the doors, a large smile plastered on my face. "I was starting to think you weren't coming back," he laughed and I shook my head, giving him a look.

"You know I'll always be here, Joe," I said, chiding him for thinking otherwise and he nodded, scratching the side of his face.

"You cool with taking sections two and three?" he asked and I nodded, waving hi to Jennifer, who'd caught my eye.

"Sounds good, old man," I grinned and he belted out laughter, taking his round of drinks to table four. Everything in the restaurant seemed more energetic to me. It was probably the buzz of conversation and the busy workplace.

"Thank God!" Shawn exclaimed as I walked through the white, swinging kitchen doors. I noticed that he was sporting a black eye and a bruise on his cheek, I didn't have to ask to know where he'd gotten those. "November, I'm really sorry about what I did the other day," he said, looking down as Jen walked in. He was quiet the whole time she was there, and I stood impatiently, resting all my weight on my back leg.

She eyed us curiously but continued on with her job and then finally, after at least two minutes of her trying to eavesdrop, left the kitchen. "I don't even know what to say. I don't know what came over me," he mumbled and I immediately felt bad, even though none of this was my fault.

"Hey, it's fine," I decided, smiling a little at him.

"For real?" he asked and I nodded, laughing off the whole situation.

"For real." He smiled and dove back into doing the dishes, his arms elbow deep in dirty water. I wrinkled my nose and took my heavy coat off, opting for my apron.

"What happened with you and Shawn?" Jen, always hungry for gossip, asked curiously as I finished taking the large order for table ten.

"Nothing," I answered vaguely, a ghost of a smile on my lips. She pouted, balancing the black circular tray on her hip bone as her short blonde bob swayed from side to side. "If you ever feel like talking I'm here," she grinned, winking at me as she walked by, both of us going in opposite directions.

I dropped some dishes off for Shawn and then carried out three different orders of food. My shoes were rubbing painfully on the back of my heel. I really needed to get some longer socks or something to prevent the dreaded blisters on my feet. By the time my shift was over, I was beat and I wanted nothing more than to go home and relax.

Of course, that's not exactly what happened.

Walking out of the restaurant once my shift had ended, I ran into Ace on his way into the diner. "There you are!" he said and I nodded, smiling.

"Here I am," I said exhaustedly.

"Have you eaten yet?" he asked and I shook my head no, leaning on him as we walked to his car.

"Awesome," he said, placing a quick kiss on my lips before he practically pushed me into the car, buckling my seatbelt for me.

"Where are we going?" I asked and he started the car, the engine rumbling quietly.

"Dinner," he said and I shook my head no.

"I look like trash, Ace," I said, putting the sun visor down so I could check my reflection in the mirror.

"No, you look good, as usual," he said and I blushed, my cheeks turning crimson.

I leaned my head against the window and was in the process of thinking everything through. My mind was tripping and stumbling over my thoughts making me antsy and confused when Ace took my hand in his making me feel instantly more relaxed, more comfortable.

Dinner—surprisingly—went pretty well. Ace was really sweet, almost peculiarly so, but in an effort to enjoy the night, I didn't question or accuse him of anything. Although maybe I should have because I had this nagging feeling in the back of my mind that he was keeping something from me, a secret of some sort.

Their oddly large scars were still on my mind, I wanted to know how they'd gotten them and what they meant. Ace hadn't mentioned anything further on the subject and I hadn't asked. I really wanted to keep the evening calm and civil. We'd eaten and talked and laughed, right down to the very end of the night when I had almost fallen asleep, exhausted from school and work.

Ace had dropped me off at home a couple hours ago and

now I was lying in bed, trying to sleep but an annoyingly prominent voice in my head was keeping me awake. It was beginning to get harder and harder to ignore, like a persistent throbbing in my skull.

"Aella," I heard suddenly and I jolted upright, searching for where the voice had come from. It sounded vaguely familiar yet at the same time I was sure I'd never heard it before. I stood up when I heard it again. The voice sounded close to me so I left my room and walked out into the kitchen area cautiously and then there it was again. It was like it was calling me, leading me somewhere and so I followed—as stupid as that might sound.

I bundled myself up in my jacket, hat, mittens, scarf and boots and grabbed my phone and key, locking the door behind me before I made my way out of my little apartment building. I wasn't quite sure how I knew where to go, but it was as if my feet were carrying themselves and I was just along for the ride. The hallway floor of my apartment creaked with every step I took, projecting the sound into the otherwise silent space.

The voice led me to that restaurant Ace had taken me to not long ago, the one where I'd met Darrius. I paused before reaching for the handle, wondering what I was going to say when I showed up by myself and out of the blue, but eventually shook my head and gave the handle a quick tug, walking through the now opened door.

I was met with a familiar view of the place but this time, I was engulfed in someone's arms. "Aella," the person breathed, like a sigh of relief, in my ear and I stiffened. When he pulled away, I realized it was Darrius. "Oh, I'm sorry. You have the wrong person," I mumbled awkwardly, giving him a tight lipped smile.

He cracked a slow grin, crossing his arms over his chest, and then regarded me with a serious expression. "What?"

he asked, his facial features hardening like I'd told a joke that he hadn't found funny. "My name's November," I said sheepishly, wondering why he was still confused about who I was. More importantly, I was wondering who 'Aella' was and why the voice in my head had led me here.

"Crap, I could kill him right about now," Darrius muttered and I looked at him funny. "Okay, this is going to sound completely crazy, but I need you to hear me out," he said and I nodded slowly, my expression morphing into one of hesitation. "Here, sit down," he said, pulling a chair out for me. I tentatively sat down and put my hands in my lap, watching him as he ran a hand through his hair.

"Like I said, this is going to seem crazy but I swear to you that it's all true, ready?"

"Yeah," I nodded, mentally preparing myself to hear some wild story about leprechauns and unicorns. I wasn't sure exactly what was wrong with Darrius, but I was going to humor him and listen to his insane story, even if it was a complete waste of my limited time.

"I'm your brother," he said and my breath caught in my throat, my heart stopping. I knew it wasn't true. I knew I was an only child, just like I knew the sky was blue and clouds were white, but something about the way he said it made me think otherwise, and my blood froze in my veins at the very thought.

It wasn't possible. It couldn't be. So why was I actually starting to believe him?

My brother? Darrius had to be completely crazy. It was undeniable at this point. "Okay," I drawled, glancing at the door, mentally calculating how fast I could escape. If I ran, I could probably make it past him safely and once I was outside I could call Ace or Charles, maybe hurry back home. I shouldn't have left in the first place. I shook my head in bewilderment.

"Stop," he said, his voice hard, devoid of any emotion.

"Stop what?" I asked, speaking through clenched teeth. "Stop looking at me like I belong in the loony bin because I don't. I'm telling you the truth and you are going to listen."

My mind screamed at me to leave, to run away from him and never come back, but at the same time I felt compelled to stay, like it was out of my control. I nodded stiffly, an action I hadn't wanted to do, and Darrius sighed while running his hands through his hair.

"I'm your brother," he repeated because he could tell I didn't believe him—or that I didn't want to at least.

"Darrius," I started, wringing my hands together in my lap nervously. I wasn't sure how to tell him that I wasn't his sister, that we weren't related.

"That's not even the best part, Aella," he said, a smug smirk on his face. He snapped his fingers and I blinked, my eyes focusing on his head. And then I screamed.

Sticking out from his hair were horns. I didn't know how else to explain them. They simply looked like short, smooth, black horns. There really weren't any other words to explain what was on his head.

I stood up abruptly, causing my chair to tip over backwards and hit the ground with a crash. I stumbled away from him, my eyes wide and locked on the horns. I blinked repeatedly while I fumbled with the door handle, checking over my shoulder to see if I had imagined what I'd seen.

"Aella," Darrius said, his shoulders dropping. "I was hoping that the horns would trigger your memory but I guess the blocks Ace used were stronger than I thought," he said thoughtfully, reaching for my arm.

"Don't touch me!" I shrunk away from him, my heart thumping in my chest.

"I won't hurt you, sis," he said, adding the last part on with a lopsided grin.

"I'm not your sister! You are not my brother, Darrius," I said, disgust evident in my voice. "I don't know what you are," I said, trying to ease the door open slow enough that he wouldn't be able to tell what I was doing until I was already gone.

The door handle was cold to the touch and rusty. I was afraid the door would creak when I pushed it open. Darrius had his back to me and he appeared to be thinking. I froze in fear when he turned around, his horns still poking out from his mess of hair.

He pinched the bridge of his nose and shrugged apologetically at me as he snapped his fingers. I had a feeling that whatever the finger snapping did couldn't be good because the last time he'd done it, horns had magically appeared on his head.

"Oh God, not again," I murmured, my eyes feeling heavy. I toppled over and Darrius darted over to catch me before I fell in a heap to the ground. I wanted to jump away from the contact because I didn't know who—or what Darrius was, but I was already unconscious.

Yeah, the finger snapping was definitely not a good thing.

# Chapter Ten

I woke up sweating and breathing heavily, my heart hammering in my chest—so loud that I could hear it in my ears. My blood turned ice cold in my veins when I saw Darrius sitting with his legs propped up on a chair and his arms crossed over his chest.

His eyes were closed and he looked like he was sleeping. His chin was resting on his arm. I rose into a sitting position, gently placing my feet on the floor. I inhaled deeply through my nose, exhaling once before standing up.

If I could get to the door, which was behind me, without waking him up then I could sneak out and go for help. I gave Darrius another glance and noticed the horns on his head, his dark hair not covering them completely. My breath caught in my throat and I had to steady myself to stop from falling backwards.

I took a tentative step forward only to have Darrius lift his head up and lock eyes with me. "Nice try," he said to my dismay and I looked upwards as if praying to the heavens that they would help me escape.

"Okay, so," he started, standing up and clasping his hands together, "I think have an idea." He grinned, putting a winter hat on top of his head, which thankfully covered his abnormal features.

"I called Ace," he told me and I looked sharply up at him, a feeling of something close to hope surfacing inside me.

"You did?" I asked slowly, wondering why he would possibly do that. It was so clearly the wrong move.

"He's the only one who can remove the blocks he put in your mind," Darrius shrugged and I gulped, lightly touching my fingers to my temple. What was he talking about? There was nothing in my mind except my thoughts—that were completely fine and normal, contrary to whatever Darrius was trying to tell me.

"What are you thinking, Aella?" he asked, cocking his head curiously to one side.

"Why do you keep calling me that?" I asked, hating the way my voice faltered. I didn't know why he thought that was my name because I remembered telling him I was November, and I wasn't even sure what I was doing here.

"It's your name," he replied, shrugging in my direction.

I shook my head in protest because my name was November. It had been since the day I was born and he knew that. "What are you feeling?" he continued, ignoring my incessant head shaking and I crossed my arms across my chest, regarding him worriedly.

"I'm confused," I admitted, my eyes trained on his feet, watching and making sure he didn't try to step towards me, "and I'm scared," I added, glancing up quickly at him to see his reaction.

"You shouldn't be. I love you, Aella. I won't hurt you," he said, his gentle smile seeming genuinely real and I swallowed the lump in my throat. "Bloody hell," he muttered, his eyes drifting over to the door behind my head.

I whipped around and saw Ace and Charles, who were both completely drenched from head to toe in dark, black-ish colored… blood? I pressed my hand over my mouth in disgust, the metallic scent immediately filling my nostrils, and backed away from them, feeling like I was going to puke.

Ace's and my eyes found each other and his gaze softened, and I watched as he dragged his hand over his face, wiping off a sheen layer of the sticky liquid. "What happened to you?" I heard Darrius ask and I turned around to face him because he sounded closer than he had been before.

"A fight," Ace said, his voice steely as his eyes locked on Darrius.

"With?" Darrius prompted, attempting to get more information out of Ace, and I watched as he sighed.

"A demon," he said and my eyes bugged out of my head, a thrill of terror coursing through me. A what?

"What's with all the blood?" Darrius asked and despite how my stomach and my mind felt, I watched him closely, trying to gauge his answer. Ace's answer to the question sounded so nonchalant, like he'd informed Darrius he'd ordered a pizza or called a taxi.

"I cut its head off."

I doubled over and my stomach heaved as I lost whatever food I'd previously eaten. Ace rushed over to me and held my hair out of my face, whispering what were supposed to be soothing things into my ear, but his words ended up just sounding creepy after his preceding statement. The blood was getting in my hair. My eyes welled up with tears and my head started spinning.

After a few minutes, he led me over to an old worn out red booth where we sat down beside each other, him staring at me, and me avoiding eye contact as best I could. The booth wasn't against a wall which allowed us to have easy access to escape on both sides, and I was contemplating jumping away from him, but thought better of it. After all, it was just Ace.

"You two being in the same room attracts a lot of demons,

you know," Ace said, notifying Darrius, who didn't look altogether surprised at the fact, as Ace gently stroked my hair. Darrius grumbled in response and then wrinkled his nose, disappearing to get Ace and Charles some fresher, nicer smelling clothes to put on. Even after they'd changed and tossed the wrecked clothing into a trash bin outside, the foul scent of blood still lingered in the air. I was almost able to see it in his hair, but it proved to be too dark to distinguish the oddly colored blood.

My head was in Ace's lap and as I said, he was stroking my hair lovingly, gently while Charles sat off to the right of us and Darrius was across the table. "Why did you call me, Darrius?" Ace murmured, his voice relaxing to my ears.

"You had her here. You could have taken her back home," he continued, not giving Darrius a chance to speak until after he'd finished properly explaining his question.

"You put blocks in her mind, Ace. I can't remove them. I need you to do it," Darrius said, his voice growing colder by the time he was done speaking.

"Why didn't you get your father to do it?" Ace asked bitterly, looking at my supposed brother darkly.

"You know better than anyone that I can't do that. I have my mission and I must complete it," Darrius retorted angrily. "By myself," he ground out the last two words and I felt Ace's body vibrate as he chuckled lightly, already having known the answer to his somewhat rhetorical question. "I need you to remove them, Ace," Darrius stated in a pleading tone, a tone that I couldn't remember Darrius using before. He didn't strike me as the kind of guy who depended on others. He seemed like a very maverick individualist.

"Why would I do that?" Ace laughed as I sat there silently, trying to comprehend the real meaning— whatever was behind the scenes, between the lines—of what they were talking about. It wasn't just about Darrius needing help. It was somehow about me too and I was dying to know how I was involved.

"You have to, Ace."

"No I don't," Ace countered, pulling me up into a sitting position so he could wrap an arm around my shoulders protectively. "She could stay like this, safe from the things that go on in our world. Have you ever given that a thought?" Ace asked, challenging Darrius's judgment. I was growing more frustrated by the second, not being able to understand what they were talking about was grating severely on my nerves.

"To keep her safe from our world would mean leaving her like this, by herself, without you, Ace. Would you be prepared for that?" Darrius asked, crossing his arms across his chest angrily. "But to truthfully answer your question, no, I haven't. You know why? Because she's my sister and I miss her. Why don't you want her to have her memories back? Because you're scared she won't love you when she finds out that our kind and your kind are enemies? Huh, Ace?" Darrius asked, his voice loud and booming, echoing throughout the restaurant. Darrius was getting mad and the air held a sort of provocative, contagious anger, and I knew Ace's temper had sparked as well.

"I'm not scared she won't love me, Darrius. You know that's not why I need her," Ace said coldly and I glanced at him sharply, something clicking in my mind. The way Ace had phrased it made it sound like it didn't matter to him whether I loved him or not, and that he couldn't be bothered to care about me either. But why would he spend all this time convincing me to date him? To trust him?

"That's not true. Obviously you're in love with her," Darrius snorted and I looked back up at Ace to see his expression.

"No, I'm not," Ace said and I couldn't help but feel a little hurt. I mean, I knew me and Ace weren't in love with each other but I still felt like we had something. After all, it seemed like it had been his sole mission to make me like him.

"Clearly," Darrius said sarcastically, gesturing to how Ace and I were sitting, while Charles cleared his throat awkwardly. I felt Ace's body stiffen beside mine and he grit his teeth together, narrowing his eyes at Darrius, the person who was claiming that we were related.

"Besides," Darrius continued thoughtfully, "you know the Archangels would never allow it."

"They wouldn't care," Ace bristled in response, and I watched as Charles glanced sharply at him, a look of skepticism and doubt on his face. Archangels? What did that even mean? And what did they have to do with me and Ace's relationship? This conversation had raised so many questions. I just needed some answers but the problem was that I didn't know who to ask.

"You know they would," Darrius insisted and Charles, even though he probably didn't want to, looked like he wanted to agree with Darrius. I focused in on Charles's face because out of all three boys, he was the easiest to read. I just wanted a hint, any hint, as to what they were discussing.

I was trying so hard to wrap my mind around what they were saying that I missed what Ace and Darrius said next, but judging by the way the air sparked with tension, they had each said something to anger the other. They glared at each other for a while, and from where I was sitting I couldn't see Ace's eyes, but Darrius's were cold and calculating, as if he was deciding what to do next.

"Remove the memory blocks, Ace," Darrius sighed, running a hand through his hair, expertly avoiding the horns that were still there. What was with the horns? It was freakishly weird and gave me chills every time I looked at them. He'd taken off his hat a few minutes ago, and he was tightly wringing it in his hands, using that as an outlet for his frustration.

"No, Darrius. I'm not going to do it," Ace said decisively,

his mind already made up and I felt his heartbeat speed up. His pulse was racing, I guessed it was because he was mad.

"Ace," Charles cleared his throat, butting into the conversation. "Maybe you should do it," he suggested and Ace turned his forceful glare on him.

"What?" he demanded, his temper rising sky high, past the clouds. I watched Charles curiously, wondering why he'd went against his best friend since birth to side with someone like Darrius, and he locked eyes with me, his Adam's apple bobbing as he swallowed.

"She'll understand," Charles said and Ace stood up, pulling me with him. Charles's green eyes darted to Ace who was making his way towards the door.

"I thought you were on my side, Charles. You know what? Just leave us alone, both of you," Ace said, taking my hand and in a second we were out the door, in his car, and on the road, driving farther and farther away from the restaurant.

"What about Charles?" I questioned, my mouth dry from not talking for what felt like a long time, shaking my head in utter bewilderment.

"Who needs him?" Ace ground out, taking my hand in his. He gently traced circles on the back of it with his thumb and then brought my hand to his lips, and kissed it softly. It was an action he usually did when I was upset, but this time it seemed like it was more for him. He laced our fingers together and kept one hand gripping the steering wheel tightly and I stared at him weirdly.

Something wasn't adding up and I was ready to make it my goal to uncover what exactly it was. I didn't answer his question as he drove, and just sighed, feeling relieved to have gotten away from Darrius yet confused and a little frightened of all three boys.

Would someone please make this a whole lot easier and just explain to me what the heck was going on?

"Ace?" I asked tentatively after a while. He'd continued driving after we'd left the restaurant and any time I tried to talk to him, he just punched the gas harder and ignored me.

"Yeah," he said, surprising me this time with an answer. It was safe to say that by now I hadn't been expecting one. I debated on what to ask him because I had so many important questions, I didn't know where to start.

"What is Darrius?" I asked tentatively because it was an odd question, the words didn't seem to quite fit in my mouth. What was he? The answer should have been simple. Darrius was a guy who was probably a little crazy, yet for some reason I could sense that it was way more complicated than that.

"Something dangerous," Ace said, his jaw clenching, his fingers turning white.

"Be serious, okay? I want real answers," I said, keeping my gaze trained on him. He glanced over at me and gave in, sighing.

"Promise me you won't freak out?" Ace gave up, running a hand through his curly black hair even though it was caked with dried blood.

"Promise," I answered, although I was a little creeped out. Was it really something that bad?

"Darrius is the Devil's offspring," Ace said, not meeting my eyes, which had bugged out of my head in an emotion close to shock. There were no words to describe what I was feeling, I had a suspicion that no one had ever been in my situation before. I stuttered, tripping and falling all over my words as I tried to form a sentence.

"You mean the Devil is his—"

"Dad," Ace finished, a crooked smile on his lips. "That is exactly what I mean."

I gaped at him, a look of pure horror on my face. My mind felt sluggish and slow, like it wasn't functioning as fast as it could, and I found it difficult to comprehend what I'd just been told. "You're his sister," Ace continued clearly avoiding my terrified and disgusted gaze, and my breath caught in my throat and I choked.

"His what?" I asked for clarification. I mean, I'd heard what he said but I didn't believe it. It couldn't be true.

"His sister," Ace said through clenched teeth.

What?

I had a whole crap load of memories of my dad and my aunt and my life before I met Ace. He was messing with me right now, right? I remembered my family and my father taking me to the diner, when I'd first met Joe and he'd hired me as a waitress. My aunt telling me stories of my mom and her artwork. I remembered it all, so Ace wasn't telling me the truth. It wasn't possible. I wanted to scream at him and yell, hit him and kick him. I needed him to see that messing with me now wasn't the best idea.

"No, that's not possible. I'm an only child, Ace. My parents are dead, I—" I had started to say hysterically when Ace stopped me.

"Your mother is dead, yes. But your dad is most certainly not, or so to speak," he said and I shook my head no wildly.

It wasn't possible, I didn't have a brother.

My mom was dead.

My dad was dead.

I didn't have a brother. The same phrase repeated itself in my brain, like a song that was stuck in my head, over and over again.

"Stop the car, please," I said calmly, gritting my teeth together painfully. I didn't want to be alone in a car with Ace anymore. He was completely insane. He was lying to me and I knew it, and I wasn't just in denial. I was certain he was lying.

"Why? What's wrong?" Ace asked but nonetheless obediently

pulled the car over to the side of the road. I hurried to unhook my seatbelt and as soon as the car stopped rolling, I hopped out, slamming the door behind me, cutting Ace off mid-speech.

The sky was dark. It was early in the morning, and there were no stars to give off any light. The moon, though, shone brightly, bathing everything in an eerie white glow. It made me want to look around and make sure I wasn't being followed. It was sinister.

"Nova," Ace said, getting out of the car.

"Stay away from me," I demanded forcefully, backing up onto the road.

"Hey, what?" Ace asked, clearly confused. Did he not see how afraid I was of him? Didn't he know that I could see through his lies? He took a step closer and I took one back, putting as much distance between us as I could. "Nova," Ace said, alarm ringing from his voice.

"Leave me alone, Ace." I was confident that the forty or so feet there was between us was enough to keep him away.

"No—" he tried again but I shook my head and yelled at him to stop talking to me. He needed to be quiet. "Listen to me, Nova! Behind you!" he roared, his voice loud and filled with panic.

I whipped around, squinting at the bright lights that shone in my eyes. I automatically understood that there was a car heading straight for me, and I knew that it was too late for them to stop, but I couldn't bring myself to move. It was like I was watching a movie, watching myself from someone else's perspective, and it wasn't until a split second before the car was going to hit me that I was sucked back into my own body, a jolt of terror going through me.

I felt a strong pair of arms go around me from behind and with a whoosh. I squeezed my eyes shut tight as I realized that I was being pulled up. I heard the steady beat of large wings pumping up and down as we rose higher in the sky.

My breath caught in my throat as I watched in amazement as the car passed under us.

Us being me and the freakishly large bird that had saved my life? I wasn't so sure about that.

My eyes were wide open as I felt my feet touch the ground lightly. I heard the thump of Ace's feet landing on the pavement as he also landed gracefully on the ground behind me and I turned around to face him incredulously, my eyes searching for something to explain what I'd just witnessed.

"You're so crazy," Ace said, his voice rushed and breathless, but sounding extremely relieved. His hands cupped my cheeks and he held my face tightly as he pressed his lips to mine, roughly kissing me. I was so surprised that it took me a few seconds to comprehend what was happening, but eventually I gave in and kissed him back, our lips moving in perfect synchronization.

"Oh God," he murmured, pressing his forehead to mine and pulling me closer, his arms around my waist. I could feel his heart beating in his chest but I didn't know why mine wasn't just as loud. Hadn't I been the one who'd almost died? As soon as my feet had touched the ground my heart had all but stopped, an odd calmness spreading through me. "That was so close, that was too close," he said softly, resting his chin on the top of my head as he hugged me so tightly that it was beginning to get hard to breathe.

"Ace, what just happened?" I asked, my throat dry and I locked eyes with him, hoping that he would help me understand.

"Does it matter?" he asked, attempting to get out of telling me, his gaze dodging away from mine.

"It matters, Ace."

"I suppose you're right," he sighed, letting his arms fall away from me. He took a step back and even though I was expecting it, the large black wings unfurling from behind him still took me by surprise and I gasped, backing away. They were huge, spanning about five feet on either side, they were covered in black feathers, long ones.

"Are you an angel?" I asked, my hand covering my open mouth.

"I— er, yeah. I am," he said, crossing his arms over his chest. "I'm an angel," he assured me, but it almost sounded like he was trying to convince himself more. He smiled suddenly and cocked his head to the side, reaching his out to lightly touch my arm. "I'm your angel, Nova," Ace softly said, his voice lowering.

"How is that even possible?" I gulped as he stepped closer. "I thought I was part Devil," I said, shuddering in disgust at the thought. Ace's hand touched my cheek lightly, his palm felt hot against my skin. It wasn't exactly every girl's dream to find out that your whole life had been a lie and you were a freak of nature.

"You're not a freak of nature," he said suddenly and I drew back harshly, aware of the fact that he'd just said exactly what I was thinking.

"How did you do that?" I demanded, touching my cheek where his hand had been, my skin still tingling from where he'd touched me.

"Do what?" he asked, playing dumb, and I clenched my jaw in annoyance.

"How did you read my mind?" I asked breathlessly, looking him up and down from head to toe.

"Perks of being an angel," he offered, shrugging nonchalantly, as if it wasn't a big deal.

"Wait, back up. So you've been able to read my mind this whole time?" I asked, shaking my head in amazement and embarrassment.

"Only when I'm touching you," he said quickly, holding his hands up innocently.

"Right. Only when you're touching me." I made a mental note to remember that.

"What else can you do?" I asked, not caring about how abnormal all this was.

"Well the flying, mind reading, and magic pretty much covers it—"

"Did you say magic? Like bippity boppity boo magic?" I asked and a smirk, his smirk, appeared on his face, as he held his hand up.

"Not exactly."

All of a sudden I was being pulled closer to him, and even when I tried to back away, I couldn't break free. "That kind of magic," he whispered in my ear once I was close enough. I gulped at his nearness and he smiled a breathtaking smile, those blue orbs of his glinting mischievously at me.

"What are the scars on your back?" I asked and he pouted, pulling away.

"Way to kill the mood," he muttered but sighed anyway, running his pale hand through his hair. "When I need to blend in with the humans, I have to hide my wings because well obviously—"

"Yeah, yeah. I get it," I said, laughing a bit despite everything and he nodded gratefully.

"But I can't make the scars disappear, I don't really know why. The place where my wings connect with my back is always showing." He shrugged like it was nothing, like the fact that he was a freaking angel didn't make things weird at all.

"But my wings are always there," he smirked, "you just can't see them most of the time," he added. I felt something go around my back and when I realized that it wasn't his arms, I jumped in surprise, which caused me to move backwards into a black, feathery wall.

"Ace!" I yelled, and he chuckled, his gorgeous face taking my breath away.

Even though I was a little confused and a little scared, I might have also been a little love-struck and I was kind of hoping that Ace would kiss me right now.

Fingers crossed, right?

"You know I can read your mind, right?" he asked, chuckling and I blushed, looking down, avoiding eye contact. He laughed loudly, and tilted my chin up, a huge Cheshire cat smile plastered on his face and it made me smile too.

Ace was leaning in to kiss me, I was probably leaning up also, when I heard someone behind us. "Don't kiss my little sister, Ace," a voice said exasperatedly, a voice that could only belong to Darrius.

"Go away," Ace said, cupping my cheeks in his hands.

"Ace," Darrius growled.

Ace grinned at me and planted a quick kiss on my lips and then turned to look at Darrius smugly. "Sorry, what?" he asked, smirking, sounding strangely confident even though Darrius was actually related to the Devil. But then again, I guess I was too. The vein on Darrius's forehead was popping out in anger, and I watched to see what Ace would do.

"What do you want?" Ace asked, his playful grin disappearing.

"My dad wants Aella to go home," Darrius answered and Ace's face paled suddenly, a drastic change from how he'd looked a second ago. He grabbed my wrist and pulled me against him, his left wing— weird, right? — circling around me.

"No."

"Ace," Darrius sighed in annoyance, pinching the bridge of his nose. "You can't just say no and expect the problem to go away. If he wants her back, he's going to get her," Darrius said, his facial features hardening in anger at Ace's stubbornness.

"Well," Ace said, wiping the beads of sweat that were

forming on his face and he looked at Darrius daringly. "Come and get us," Ace sneered, snapping his fingers. With a whoosh, Ace and I were no longer standing beside Darrius on the road, we were somewhere else entirely. I felt a little breathless as I blinked to clear my vision and take a long, fascinated look around.

"Get in," Ace said, gesturing to his car. I didn't question it as I climbed into the passenger seat, buckling up my seatbelt. Whatever Ace had just done had worked. Darrius was no longer in sight.

"Where are we going?" I asked Ace curiously as he punched the gas. "Far away," he answered vaguely.

Far away? What about my house? My aunt? My job?

"It will all be fine, Nova," Ace said and I studied my feet.

"How come you call me that? Why don't you call me Aella?" I asked and he glanced over sharply.

"I don't know," he mumbled, bringing his attention back to the road.

"Should we get Charles?" I asked quickly and Ace looked at me incredulously, probably wondering why I would ever want him here, but even though he'd gone against Ace, he'd been proven right, hadn't he? I knew the truth now and I had forgiven Ace. I understood.

"Why?"

"Because Charles can help us. He's still your best friend Ace," I said and Ace furrowed his brow, pondering what I'd said.

"I guess you're right," he sighed, reluctantly grabbing his cellphone from his pants pocket. He dialed Charles and made arrangements to pick him up from his house in twenty minutes. I sat back in my seat and tried to relax my tense muscles, but I felt like at any moment something was going to jump out at me. I closed my eyes and let my head fall against the window.

Ace reached for my hand but I pulled out of his grip lightly, not wanting him to know what I was thinking, not wanting him to know that I was scared.

What happened to peace and quiet?

# Chapter Eleven

For the rest of the car ride, we were silent. I was still trying to process everything and Ace was giving me some time to do just that. It was quiet until Charles got in the car.

"Let's go to Hawaii."

Ace sighed and pursed his lips, staring straight ahead at the road. "Charles, we're not going to Hawaii," Ace said exasperatedly. "And before you ask, we're not going to Cuba, Jamaica or Mexico either," Ace added quickly, naming off all the tropical places he could think of off the top of his head. Charles's shoulders sank in disappointment. "We need to go somewhere inconspicuous and isolated," Ace announced, and I turned to look at him expectantly.

"Where?" I asked but surprisingly he shook his head no.

"You don't get to know."

"What?" I demanded, my blood beginning to boil.

"I said I'm not telling you," Ace said and my jaw dropped, my eyes widening.

"Well why not?" I asked after he didn't offer any sort of explanation.

"Because, Aella, your father would easily be able to get into your thoughts. By the time we got where we were going there would already be an ambush waiting for us,"

Ace said, startling me with the use of the foreign sounding name. I briefly wondered if by me asking him why he didn't use my real name, it had made him reconsider and decide to stop calling me November. I was hoping that wasn't the case because I liked having one thing from my life that I could hold onto.

"Did you know that the name Aella means "whirlwind" in Greek?" Charles piped up from the backseat again.

"Cool," I mumbled, not quite sure why he'd told us that. Of course, he didn't waste the opportunity to explain.

"Kind of like us right now on our whirlwind of an adventure to nobody-except-Ace-knows-where-land," he said and I rolled my eyes.

A look of worry surfaced on my face and Ace smiled gently, but kept his eyes on the road. "I promise he won't get you, Nova. I'll protect you," Ace said and Charles snorted but didn't saying anything.

I nodded and sank back into the seat, staring out the window. I smiled inwardly, glad that Ace hadn't stopped calling me November for the rest of my life. Even though the name was weird and long, it was still comforting and familiar.

What a wild day.

It was taking all my energy to try and wrap my head around what had happened today—not to mention the fact that I'd actually experienced all the exhausting things I was thinking of—and I wanted so badly to close my eyes and go to sleep.

But I forced my eyes open, even though they were stinging from tiredness, and watched for any road signs that would help me decipher where we were going. "Go to sleep, Nova," Ace murmured, and I remembered that he was holding my hand, thus allowing him access to my thoughts.

It sounded so weird to even think that he could read my mind. Ace chuckled a little and I smiled sleepily, pulling my hands from his. I don't know about you, but I like to keep my thoughts private. Ace sighed and rested his hand on his thigh, keeping the other on the steering wheel, driving to God knows where.

"So," Charles started, startling me and I jumped in my seat unexpectedly. I had completely forgotten he was there—I don't think I've ever heard Charles be that quiet for so long ever since I'd met him.

"I was thinking... the Bahamas?"

Lying next to Ace on the bed in the hotel room, his arm wrapped around my stomach possessively, I finally had time to think. I wasn't even worried about him reading my thoughts because he was out cold, snoring softly. Charles was doing something similar, but he was also mumbling things in his sleep, incoherent words that didn't even sound like English.

I'd woken up ten minutes ago and had just laid here, my mind going a million miles per minute. It was all so confusing to me. I couldn't wrap my head around it. I felt completely and utterly overwhelmed and there was absolutely nothing I could do about it. It made me feel so utterly powerless and I twisted around slowly, turning to face the boy sleeping soundly next to me. I carefully examined his angelic facial features—no pun intended.

I lifted my hand to gently trace the lines of his face and I gasped as an indescribable feeling washed over me, seizing control over my body. I jerked my hand back reflexively, not that it helped, and sat up, Ace's arms falling away from me.

My eyes opened wide and I gasped again. It was as if someone had dumped a bucket of ice water over my head. I felt so cold, chills crawling up my back. And then all of a sudden I was being sucked away from the hotel room, from the bed, from Charles and from Ace.

I could hear Ace speaking loudly but it sounded distant, like a dream.

And then it was gone, I was somewhere else completely different.

The walls of the hotel room fell away and were replaced with brick, the bed beneath me turned to stone and everything else was gone. I was in an alleyway by the looks of it, but where? How had I gotten here?

"Seth," I heard an unfamiliar voice say. I quickly stood up, brushing off my pants, and looked around to see where the voice was coming from. "Uriel." I turned around to see Ace, glaring at something behind me.

"Ace!" I exclaimed in relief, hurrying over to stand beside him but he didn't even glance in my direction.

"Did you do it yet?" the man asked, the one Ace was talking to, and Ace began to shake his head no.

"She doesn't trust me enough yet. Give it two more weeks, Uriel, and then it'll be done," Ace answered and I watched him, puzzled.

"Ace?" I asked, waving my hand in front of his face. Nothing.

"You don't have much time, Seth. It's dangerous enough as it is for me to be talking to you. I can't get caught. You know what that would mean, right?"

"Yeah, yeah. You'll end up like me," Ace grumbled, crossing his arms over his chest impatiently.

"You must hurry," Uriel said and Ace nodded in understanding.

"Did you get the book yet?" Ace questioned and the man nodded, walking out of the shadows towards Ace. He quickly looked around and then slipped something from under his robe, passing it to Ace. It was an ancient worn out book, the pages were bent and frazzled. I wanted to examine the aged book, to run my fingers over the faded cover.

I tore my eyes away from the hardcover book that looked so interesting and glanced up at Ace, still attempting to figure out what was going on here. I couldn't read his expression as he stared down at the old book. "I have to go," Uriel said suddenly. Before I could even get one last look at him, he snapped his fingers and then vanished, leaving Ace and me alone in the alleyway. He started walking and I hurried to keep up, walking beside him as he turned onto the deserted street. We were in Brookhaven, I realized with a jolt. All the way back in Brookhaven...

Ace pulled his hood over his head, hiding his messy black hair underneath, and hunched his shoulders. I feebly tried to get his attention and then eventually gave up, letting him walk away from me. "Nova?" I heard distantly and I looked up, glancing around frantically.

"What's wrong with her?" Charles asked, his voice getting louder by the second.

I blinked in confusion and then I was back.

Back in the hotel room, back on the bed, back in Ace's arms. The two boys were leaning over me worriedly and I sat up, nearly smashing my forehead into Charles's, seeing as how his head was ever so close to mine. "You okay?" Ace asked suddenly and I looked up at him, pulling my attention away from Charles.

"But you were..." I trailed off after receiving a weird look from Ace and then shook my head to clear my thoughts. Something about what I'd just seen had been strangely eerie, unnerving if anything.

"What just happened?" Charles asked loudly, interrupting mine and Ace's exchange of glances.

"I don't know," I admitted, thinking hard about what I just saw.

I had witnessed Ace taking part in something that looked like a drug deal—or a book deal I guess you could call it. I'd seen a mystery man who knew Ace by his angel name and I'd overheard Ace and him talking about a girl and yet I only seemed to have one comment.

I didn't know Ace had such a strong passion for reading.

"You good?" Charles asked me quietly as Ace exited the room, his phone in hand. I stared after him for a moment, wanting to talk to him, but quickly focused back on Charles.

"Yeah," I responded just as softly as him, speaking so low to make sure that Ace didn't hear. "I'm fine," I smiled reassuringly, even though on the inside my stomach was twisted in one big knot.

Charles smiled back, his dimples giving him his famous boyish look, and he pulled me into a hug. "You scared me last night," Charles breathed and I nodded, moving back to look at him, his vibrant jade colored eyes boring into me.

"Sorry," I shrugged apologetically, even though it hadn't exactly been my fault.

He shook his head and squeezed me tighter one more time and then let go just as Ace walked back into the room. "You have wings too, right Charles?" I asked curiously and he nodded, smiling proudly as if having them was an achievement of the highest order.

I hadn't really talked to Charles, one of my only friends, about him being an angel. I guess I'd just been so caught up with everything else. I sighed, feeling a little bad and vowed to sit down and talk with him once this mess had settled down. I looked over at Ace whose teeth were clenched in frustration or anticipation, I wasn't sure which one, and waited for him to say something. When he didn't, I spoke out, wanting to help him.

"What's wrong?" I asked him, moving closer to gently place my hand on his shoulder. He jumped away as if I had startled him and I lowered my hand to my hip, balancing my weight on one foot awkwardly.

"Sorry, Nova," Ace said, sighing, rubbing his forehead tiredly, as if he was stressed about something. "We have to go," he added and Charles looked up sharply, obviously because Ace had neglected to tell him before me.

"Go where?" he beat me to asking the question.

"We don't have time for me to explain. We just have to get going," Ace muttered agitatedly, thumping his foot impatiently while glaring at Charles. There was something wrong. Anyone could have seen that, but I wished that he would tell me what was going on with him.

"Why?" Charles started to ask but Ace silenced him with a look of pure hatred, a fire burning so hot it was blue. I shied away from him unnoticeably, crossing my arms over my chest.

"Stop asking questions and do what I tell you," Ace whispered harshly into his ear making Charles's back stiffen in annoyance.

Charles immediately stopped talking and walked past Ace, heading for the car. Ace looked up at me, a foreign emotion in his eyes, which vanished as soon as I began trying to decipher it. Ace stepped over to me, taking my face in his hands and pressed a kiss to my lips. It lasted twenty seconds, if not less but still felt altogether too short.

I opened my mouth to speak but Ace hurried out the door, not even waiting for me. The way Ace was acting was starting to mess with my mind and make me second guess everything he did. Plus, there was what I'd seen last night in my dream vision thing. I stood there silently for a minute, before walking out the door after him. I climbed in the front seat of the car and the boys' hushed angry voices silenced immediately.

It was odd, I have to admit. The car ride to wherever we were headed got even weirder. I could feel that something was wrong, the tension in the air crackling like a live wire. Ace didn't even glance over at me and Charles said nothing—absolutely nothing. If it was any other day I might have been rejoicing but not now. Right now I needed Charles' easy conversation and Ace's absentminded hand holding.

"What's wrong with you two?" I demanded as the car rolled to a stop. They both ignored me, their eyes focused so intently on something else, they probably hadn't even heard me speak. I searched for what they were staring at and, for once, my eyes didn't fail me. I saw clear as day the focus of their attention.

I recognized it, the person, as soon as I laid eyes on him. He was in that vision I'd had last night. His name was... Mar-something? No that was wrong, not even close, November. I wracked my brain for the name but I just couldn't think of it.

"Get out of the car, Nova," Ace said and I turned to look at him incredulously.

"What? No!" I said, alarmed, panic invading my head.

"Get out of the car, please," Ace said, his eyes filling with pain.

"Are you insane?" I asked bluntly, pleading with him.

Ace sighed and shut his eyes tightly and then climbed out of the car, coming around to my side. "No," I said as Ace opened my door. He seized hold of my wrists and pulled me out forcefully.

"Nova, listen to me, okay?" Ace said, his hands cupping my cheeks, making me look at him. "He won't hurt you,"

Ace started and I glanced doubtfully at Uriel, the name popping up in my head.

"Wait, you know him?" Ace asked, his thoughts clouding and he furrowed his brow. I couldn't even begin to imagine what was going through his head right now, if only the mind-reading trick worked both ways.

"We've met before, last night actually. Aella, I presume?" I nodded at Uriel and Ace's eyes bugged out of his head.

"Charles and I were with her all night, Uriel."

"We met in your memories, Seth. Granted we couldn't speak to each other because I had to follow according to the memory, but we met," Uriel said and I looked at him in confusion although what he was saying was somewhat true. But I didn't think he could see me yesterday. I thought I had been invisible to them. Uriel hadn't even looked at me once.

Ace shook his head to clear it as Uriel walked over. "He's going to take you somewhere, but don't be frightened. You'll be in good hands," Ace assured me while Uriel attempted to compose his facial features that were threatening to burst out laughing.

Uriel grasped me by the forearms and shoved me forward hard, and I stumbled a few steps, ending up in front of the brick wall that belonged to the nearby building. "Actually, Seth, there has been a change of plans," Uriel said, pulling something metal from under his peculiar robe.

"What?" Ace asked, his face falling as he glanced at what was in Uriel's hand. The car door slammed as Charles climbed out but I didn't even look up. My eyes were focused on Ace's face.

"Kill her. Oh, and Seth?" Uriel started, waiting for Ace to acknowledge him, and Ace looked at him sharply, hopefully. "Please don't dawdle, I don't have all day, you know."

Ace looked at the gun that was in his hands now and up at me, his eyes filled with despair. I could see it plainly though

I was some twenty feet away. "Ace don't—," my voice broke and Uriel begun to speak over me. I simply didn't have the courage to speak louder right now.

"You want this don't you, Seth? Or would you rather spend the rest of your miserable life damned in hell?" Uriel said, his voice seeping with persuasiveness. I could tell it was affecting Ace's decision and he glanced back at the gun, raising it slightly and looked at me.

"Ace?" I asked quietly, because I knew he could hear me, but his resolve hardened.

"Do it or you'll never get the chance," Uriel said, his arms crossed over his chest. I noticed that he looked much older than Ace, his face was lined with wrinkles and his hair was graying at the roots.

"Nova, I'm so sorry," Ace said and I couldn't believe he was even considering it. That he would even think about going through with it. How could he do this to me? After all this time we'd spent together? He'd been convincing me to trust him from the very first day I'd known him, and this is what I got for letting him in?

"Seth!" Uriel roared and before I knew it, a gun shot rang off, echoing loudly in my ears.

You've got to be freaking kidding me.

# Chapter Twelve

I've never wondered what it would be like to have a guardian angel, and yet, I can't imagine it being quite like this. 'Guard' means to protect, therefore 'guardian' means protector. And yet, it was kind of the opposite in this case because my supposed 'guardian' angel had just *tried* to kill me.

Tried being the keyword in that sentence. Charles, bless his heart, had jumped in front of me—well I guess he flew, or had he run over? I suppose it didn't really matter at this point.

"Oh my God," I gasped, covering my mouth in horror. I fell to my knees beside him, grabbing his hand in mine and our eyes met, his filled with pain.

"Damn," he muttered, wincing in pain. "I forgot how much getting shot hurt," he rasped and I let out a short, barky laugh despite the tears on my cheeks.

"Hey, don't cry," he said softly, reaching up shakily to wipe away the little droplets of water sliding down my face. "I'm going to be fine," he smiled at me. The way he said it so certainly was enough to help me understand.

"Perks of being an angel?" I guessed, using Ace's phrase, relief washing over me as I held his hand.

"I'm not an angel, November. And neither is Ace. Not

anymore," he said darkly and I looked at him in confusion. His scarlet blood was soaking into my clothes and pooling around us on the ground, staining the dirt a crimson red.

At that moment, I glanced up at Ace who was staring at the gun in his hand, dumbfounded and Uriel was nowhere to be seen. Ace's eyes met mine and he watched me for a moment, as if he didn't even recognize me, and then stumbled over to Charles and me, wild and desperate. He could see the distrust and anger etched onto my face as I got to my feet clumsily and backed away. "Nova, you don't understand," Ace pleaded with me.

"You tried to kill me," I breathed, my mind not comprehending the statement I'd just made.

Ace had tried to kill me? It didn't sound possible. The words didn't fit together in my head. Ace would never do that, not to me. But how could I deny what I'd just seen?

"Listen to me," he begged, his eyes hopeless and untamed. He cupped my cheeks in his hands, forcing me to look at him. "I love you." I wanted so badly to go back in time, to when that statement felt true, to when I could say the same thing back. Now, I knew better than to believe his lies. I drew back from him, horrified and disgusted by him, wishing I could just disappear, be anywhere but here.

"You tried to kill me," I repeated slowly, trying to get it in my head, a look of fear taking up permanent residence on my facial features.

I stared at this person, this thing, I'd come to know and love and fathomed that I didn't recognize him. He wasn't the same person I'd fallen in love with because the Ace I knew would never have done that, not in a million years, not to me. "I'm sorry," he said desperately but how was one measly apology supposed to fix things? He had just tried to shoot me, and for what? His own personal gain?

I turned so my back was facing him and started to walk

away, tears stinging my eyes and my hands curled into tight fists. "Please wait!" he called, looking between me and Charles, deciding if he should go after me or help who he'd just shot. I risked a glance back and saw Ace's distraught face as he hurried over to Charles, dropping to his knees beside his best friend. I supposed I should be glad that he didn't come after me. Ultimately it would simply give me more time to figure out what I was going to do.

Choking back my unwanted tears, I hurried along the sidewalk, not wanting Ace to catch me. "We're fallen angels, November," Charles yelled, his voice strong and booming considering the state he was in as I left. It only took three seconds, maybe less, for the words to register in my mind.

The string of words that formed a small, simple sentence came like a slap to the face. It wasn't just what Charles had said. There was a deeper meaning behind his words that landed sharp painful blows to my skull. Well, that's what it felt like. I stumbled forwards, holding my head in between my hands, as memories washed over me.

My memories, the ones that were concrete, not the figments of Ace's imagination that he'd planted there, the real ones. Countless memories hit me. It was like I was reliving my entire life. But technically I was, wasn't I?

I saw myself from someone else's eyes. My brother, my dad, my home, my life before I'd been sent up to Earth and my brain had been wiped. These were my personal recollections and I wondered briefly how anyone could possibly think they had a right to steal those from me.

After they stopped, after I remembered everything, I stood up and looked around, hurrying off into the shadows of the morning. It felt empowering. There were no other words for it. I knew who I was, what I could do, what I was meant to do and the best part of the whole situation was that my brain was so overloaded. All my thoughts of Ace temporarily disappeared. I choked on hysterical laughter as a memory of me and Darrius, my brother, surfaced in my head.

I had been an ugly kid.

I was headed home. It was a little unnerving that I had to go to... well, Hell, but I'd been there before, right? That was my home, where I was supposed to live. It wasn't as hard as I thought it would be to find one of the many gateways. As I went through, I'd looked behind me to make sure no one would see.

You'd be surprised at how easy getting down there was. The doors were all over the world, at least two in very city. And I knew every single one of them. It was like they were calling me. I could practically hear the Earth as I walked on it, begging me to return to where I was from.

So now here I was, at a place that resembled a castle, standing on the doorstep. I must have looked so small in comparison to the house. For a moment I could see myself from someone else's eyes. I shook my head and raised my hand to knock, knock on this door that I remembered vividly from my memories. There was no need, though, because the door swung open by itself.

"Nova, wait!" I heard Ace yell and I whipped around, his presence surprising me. "How did you find me, Ace?" I asked, sighing in anger and annoyance.

"I followed you," he stated simply and I shook my head in vexation.

"Why would you do that?" I demanded, shooting a glance over my shoulder at the place that was waiting impatiently for me to enter.

"Because, Nova. I love you," he pleaded, his raven colored hair a messy mop on his head, and I scowled.

"Oh, that's rich," I said sarcastically, turning to go inside.

"Nova!" he grabbed my arm and spun me around.

"Let go of my arm, Ace," I said, fearing that he'd kill me now that he had the chance.

"Oh God, Nova. I wouldn't do that," Ace said his voice filled with horror and I ripped my limb from his tight grasp.

"Is it really that unbelievable for me to think you would, Ace? You tried to do it yesterday," I said guardedly, because even though my dad was immortal, I was most certainly not, and he shook his head no, back and forth frantically.

"I wasn't going to, I swear. But then Uriel got in my head and—"

"Save it for someone who cares," I said and backed up a step, inching closer to the looming castle doors.

"Once you go in there, Nova, he won't let you out," Ace warned and I rolled my eyes. He was so plainly reaching for a reason to make me go with him back up and I knew that, vowing to not fall into his pool of lies.

I'd already figured out that there was no shallow end where you could wade in and hurry back out once you got too cold. No, with Ace once you fell in, there was no coming out. You would drown before you managed to claw your way back to the shore. His pool of deception wasn't even a pool anymore. It was more like the Atlantic Ocean.

"Shut up," I muttered distractedly as I took another step closer.

"Aella, stop," he said, surprising me with the use of my real name.

"Ace, seriously?" I turned to him, anger burning in my veins.

"You don't get to make this decision for me. This is my home. My family is here. It's my choice whether or not I go inside and see them, so back off," I said. He looked a little taken aback by my outburst but he regained control of his facial features quickly and took my hand in his.

"I promise I'm telling the truth. I love you," Ace said and I watched him closely.

"Are you being genuine, Ace? Are you for real?" I questioned, searching his gaze for anything that would tell me otherwise, a small part of me wanting to believe him.

"Yes, Nova, I'm for real," Ace smiled and I glanced back at my home, where my family was. When Ace had told me not to go inside, well he was probably right. Once anyone stepped foot in this house they couldn't leave without my dad's permission. It was a pain really, but I had managed just fine.

"I need to see them, Ace. I need to see Darrius at least. He's my brother. I just have to," I murmured, taking a step back. "I'm sorry," I mouthed to him and he squeezed my hand tighter like he was trying to hold on.

"I thought I heard your voice," I heard Darrius say from behind me in relief and I turned to see him standing inside the doorway.

"Hey," I smiled, going in for a hug.

"November, please," Ace said, his voice thick with emotion. I turned just in time to watch a single tear run down his cheek as he watched me walk inside my house.

"Goodbye, Ace," I said, smiling even though tears were pricking my eyes.

"No, I won't let you go," he said, wiping at the tear that was rolling slowly down his face. In two seconds he was next to me, inside my house, knowing full well what that would mean.

"Are you insane?" I asked, my mouth hanging open.

"I—"Ace started, looking at the door in disbelief. He looked at me then, his eyes filled with love for me and a little bit of fear as he realized what he'd just done.

"No," I said helplessly, trying to push Ace out of the house. He needed to leave. He couldn't be in here. I wouldn't be able to help him. Why was he such an idiot?

"Oh, come on, Aella. You know that won't do anything," Darrius shrugged and I cursed under my breath, turning back to Ace.

"You must be crazy," I told Ace, frustrated with him. Actually, no. Frustrated wasn't the right word. I was downright furious. The corners of his lips turned up in a slow, agonizing smile as he looked at me.

"Crazy in love with you," he said and I scowled turning to my brother, ignoring Ace's statement.

"We need to get him out of here," I said and Darrius gave Ace a lazy once over, thoroughly unimpressed by what he was seeing.

"We could just let Dad kill him and be done with it," Darrius suggested, but I shook my head no quickly.

"That is not an option," I said steely, catching my brother's eye.

He nodded reluctantly after a bit and I turned to Ace, whose face had paled immensely. It was almost like I was staring at a ghost. "Ace, you'll be fine," I said reassuringly, touching his arm lightly. He swallowed the lump in his throat, his Adam's apple bobbing, and smiled at me.

"Well," he started quietly, "at least I get to spend my last day alive with you." I shook my head, my eyes filling with tears.

"You're not going to die," I sniffed, wiping my eyes as I tried my hardest not to cry.

"I thought you didn't care," Ace said, his gaze boring into me, looking and searching for something that he knew he'd find.

"I don't, not really," I lied easily, attempting a façade of indifference. He narrowed his eyes because he knew I was lying. I mean, of course I cared. Feelings didn't just disappear overnight. You could pretend as much as you wanted but that's all it would be... pretend. I was in love with him, and it didn't matter that he had tried to kill me. He'd explained what had happened. It didn't matter that he had been faking our relationship until a few days ago, as long as he loved me now. That was what mattered.

"Then you won't care if I go turn myself in to your dad right now?" he asked daringly, watching me with those dark eyes of his.

"No," I said, biting my lip to stop it from trembling.

"I'll be off then," he said, probably faking his dejectedness, turning away from me. He started to walk down a random corridor. He had absolutely no idea where he was headed, but I knew, and that was why I had to stop him.

"Ace!" I yelled in a frustrated manner, my emotions too prominent in my voice. He looked back at me with a smirk planted on his lips and he came back over, his arms circling around my waist, pulling me up against his body.

"I knew it," he breathed, his mouth hovering closer to mine.

"Whatever," I answered cheekily, letting him kiss me. He pressed his lips against mine softly and I smiled, tangling my fingers in his hair.

"Guys?" Darrius rolled his eyes, coughing awkwardly, and I pushed Ace away quickly, scratching my head in embarrassment.

"Ah, sorry," I said sheepishly and he shrugged after a bit of glaring in Ace's direction. My brother just had to ruin moments like these, didn't he? I turned to look at Ace and he dropped me a wink, exactly like the first time I'd met him. Chills crept up my back and I shook my head, the smallest hint of a smile hiding beneath the surface. Unfortunately, I soon realized that Ace was not the reason for the chills, it was something else entirely.

"Well, hello there," a deep booming voice said from behind me, echoing around the room. It made my blood freeze and my heart completely stop, only to start beating again with renewed force, adrenaline pumping into my system.

I closed my eyes tightly, preparing myself for who I was about to see. For some reason, as I turned, the details of the dark gray walls stood out to me. I saw every nook and every cranny, every line and every speck of dirt. My heart was beating loudly in my ears as I came face to face with the one man, other than my brother, who I'd known since birth.

My father.

I just love family reunions, don't you?

"Dad," I breathed staring at him.

I looked at his face, identifying all the features that were so familiar to me. His jet black hair curled around his ears like Ace's and there was a little bit of stubble on his chin. He was usually clean shaven, but he probably hadn't had time to shave today. His white skin was similar to that of my own, perhaps a tad darker, and his light green eyes stared back at me. "I see you've brought a guest," he remarked humorlessly, looking Ace up and down thoroughly disappointedly.

"I—"

"A fallen angel, really Aella?" he said and I clenched my teeth in annoyance, my father's hatred for everything was a little frustrating. Yes, he was the Devil, but he played the part a little too well for my liking. "I'm going to have to kill him, you know that?" he told me and my eyes shot open in alarm, although I should have been expecting it.

"No, just let him go," I said, stepping between Ace and my father bravely, but I probably looked anything but.

"Let him go? That's not how we run things here in Hell, sweetheart," my dad smiled cruelly, stepping around me. I curled my hands into fists, my fingers turning white and I ground my teeth together, trying to stop myself from saying something that I would regret. My dad took another step and my brother saw what I was about to do, even before I did it.

"Aella," Darrius warned as I shoved my dad backwards, pushing him away.

"Get out of my way," he said in exasperation, locking eyes with me.

"No," I challenged, but Ace grabbed my arm, turning me around to face him.

"Don't be stupid. Let him kill me," he breathed quietly and I turned my anger on him, my emotions running wild in my head.

"Do you even know what you're saying?" I yelled loudly, my dad proceeding to annoyingly shush me. "You'll be dead and I'll have no one," I sniffed, watching him carefully for his reaction.

"I know that," he swallowed, "but I don't want you to do something you'll regret."

"If you give up without even trying, I swear to God Ace, the only thing I'll regret is ever having loved you," I hissed harshly, the threat hanging between us in the air for a moment. He looked surprised by my words but his gaze hardened, as well as his resolve.

"I'm not going to let you get hurt, November," Ace said stubbornly, his gaze level with mine. I wanted so badly to make him see this from my point of view, show him how utterly stupid he was being.

"This is touching and all, but I have things to do, chaos to cause, people to kill and all that jazz, so what's it going to be Aella?" my dad said, waiting impatiently for me to make a decision, and I looked at him with pure hatred.

"What is wrong with you?" Anger was pumping through my veins, fueling me and giving me the courage to stand up to my father.

"Many things," was his dry remark as he inspected the dirt under his fingernails.

"You're my father," I said, tears threatening to spill as he watched me emotionlessly, his eyes holding a look of indifference.

"Yes, and?" he asked, waiting for me to continue with my explanation.

"And I'm asking you not to kill him," I said, disgust finding its way into my voice.

"Enough, Aella. You're being foolish and he needs to die. Now move—"

"Do you really not care?" I asked, tears stinging the back of my eyes. Why did he have to act like such a heartless monster?

"That's correct, Aella. I really don't," he said, his gaze lingering on Ace as I spoke. I could see it on his face. His evident revulsion at the fallen angel in his home and it only managed to make me that much more vexed and my resolve that much stronger.

"Well," I sniffed, looking my dad in the eyes. They were the exact same color as mine, a pale green, and I knew that he was the parent I'd gotten them from. "If he dies then I want you to kill me too," I said and his eyebrows shot up disbelievingly, skeptically.

"You don't mean that," he said, crossing his arms over his chest.

"I think she does," Ace said, surprising me by speaking up, He stepped forward out of the shadows and took ahold of my hand. My dad's eyes hardened in hatred as he watched Ace.

"Dad, please? You're my father and yes, you're the devil, but we're family. I love you. Don't you love me?" I asked and his eyes bore daggers into mine, his lips staying sealed shut. "Don't you love Darrius?" I asked when he didn't respond to the first question and my brother gave me that look, the one where he knew I'd dragged him into something he wouldn't be able to get out of later.

My dad's face had barely changed, remaining as impassive as stone. So I kept pushing, trying to find his weak spot. And then an idea came to me, a bright light bulb illuminating in my mind and I crossed my arms, cocking my head to the side. It was probably a horrible idea. It could end very badly for Ace and myself, but it was still an idea and at the moment, it was the only one I had. "Didn't you care about mom?" I asked quietly and saw him frown even more, a new emotion appearing in his eyes.

My first thought was rage. He was probably furious with me for bringing up such a touchy subject, but then something happened that made me doubt that considerably. I was altogether amazed, shocked and astonished because I didn't think I'd ever seen this specific thing happen before, ever in my life. My mom had been human and she'd died when I was born, that part of the web of lies had been true. But, don't they always say the best lies are the ones kept as close to the truth as possible?

I didn't know her name. My dad never talked about her, and when I said never, I meant *never*. Anytime I used to bring her up in conversation, my dad shut me down and refused to speak. Same with Darrius. Speaking of my dear brother, I glanced over at him and I immediately felt like I'd crossed a line, a thick line that was painted bright red telling me to stop before I made a mistake. Well, it was far too late for that.

But Darrius and I were both looking at the same thing. Our eyes filled with amazed bewilderment as we watched a single tear roll down my father's cheek. Ace's grip on my hand tightened in angst but I couldn't look away from the small droplet of water as it fell off his face, splashing on his shirt.

"I did love your mother," he said and I breathed in sharply, my eyes widening. "She was the love of my life. But I am the devil, Aella, you understand that, right? I don't get what I want. I am incapable of loving," he said and I shook my head no, tears welling up in my eyes.

"You have a family, Dad. We're here for you," I said, hoping Darrius wouldn't jump in and say something stupid to ruin the moment. It was so like Darrius to do something like that, wreck a perfectly good thing; but I was too close to persuading our father to let Ace and I go for him to mess it up.

"Please. Let us go," I threw in after a moment of letting my words sink in, mentally crossing my fingers, sending up a silent prayer from the depths of hell all the way to wherever prayers went when they were said. He looked at me once, our eyes locking and then he sighed, his shoulders drooping.

"Go, then," he said, but everyone was much too stunned to comprehend. So we, Ace, Darrius and I, stood there staring at him. "Go!" he shouted, abruptly yanking all of us from our stupefied silence.

"Thank you," I whispered before grabbing Ace's hand and dragging him swiftly through the doors, out of the house. It wasn't like a rush of fresh air like you would expect walking out of building. No, it was a feverishly hot atmosphere, seeping into our skin as we made our way down the concrete steps, starting down the long, winding path. Ace wrapped his arm around my shoulder and we kept walking, far away from this horrid place, as I thought a million thoughts, wanting to say a million words.

I guess that even in the darkest of places, the places haunted with shadows and gloom, light can still shine, find its way in even if it's through the smallest of cracks. The coldest of hearts, untouched by feelings of warmth, can still love, even if it doesn't seem possible. I suppose that love will always prevail, it *really is* a thousand times stronger than hatred and it was so easy to say, to understand, now that I'd experienced it firsthand. And believe me when I said it was wonderful.

"Charles!" I exclaimed happily, running over to throw my arms around him. It was good to see his familiar, happy face and I sighed in relief. What an emotional roller coaster this whole situation had been. I didn't think I could take anymore.

"You got her back?" Charles asked, somewhat doubtfully, but nonetheless hugged me back. His tight hold on me was comforting and he gave me one last squeeze before stepping back.

"Yeah, I did," Ace said, smiling as he stared at the back of my head.

"Are you okay?" I asked Charles, ignoring Ace's statement, lifting Charles's shirt up to look at the bullet wound that had been there two days ago.

"Nova," Ace coughed, glaring at me for 'taking off Charles' shirt' as he had put it.

"It's better?" I asked, poking the small white scar. It didn't seem possible that the wound that had been pouring blood could be reduced to that so quickly. But then again, anything was possible ever since Ace had come into my life.

"All better," he gave me two thumbs up, smiling widely. He pushed his blond hair back and away from his face as he watched me intently, making me the slightest bit uncomfortable. I felt Ace's hand gently take mine and a permanent smile spread across my features.

"Your hair looks longer," Charles finally remarked

thoughtfully and I rolled my eyes, playfully swatting his arm. He was absolutely ridiculous.

"I was gone for two days, not two years," I said laughing.

"I know, but it still felt like forever," he said, his gaze lingering a little too long on my pale pink lips before he looked up at Ace.

"You're lucky she forgave you," Charles said, frowning in Ace's direction.

"I know," Ace said.

As the two boys conversed, I let my mind wander to my dad. Would he change his mind and come after us? Ace looked back over at me, wrapping his arm around my shoulders to pull me close to his chest. "Hey, don't worry. We're safe now," Ace said, reading my thoughts and I sighed, but there was nothing I could do about the constant worrying. It would remain for a few weeks, at least until I was convinced I was safe.

"How'd you guys get away?" Charles asked and I smiled at Ace knowingly.

"He let us go," I informed him and his eyebrows shot up disbelievingly, skepticism written all over his face. My thoughts were in accord with Charles' because that had been the weirdest most astonishing thing I'd ever experienced and I looked at Ace to see what he would say, but Charles' posed a question first.

"You escaped the Devil?"

"No, we didn't have to because he let us go," Ace said forcefully, backing me up on what I'd told Charles, and he snorted derisively at him. He shook his head in amazement and slumped against the brick wall of a nearby building, watching me and Ace.

"You are one lucky guy, Ace," Charles said, shaking his head like he couldn't believe everything we just told him. Heck, I wouldn't believe us either.

"I know," Ace repeated surely and I leaned into him happily. "So what's the plan?" Charles asked and I knew he had already made up his mind on what he wanted to do. I could have easily guessed that it was some sort of tropical vacation, Charles wasn't a hard person to read.

"We're not going to Hawaii," Ace said and I laughed, smirking contently at Ace from the side.

"We could," I shrugged, contradicting him, and Ace fixed me with a stern glare, but before he could say something, Charles jumped to interrupt.

"See, two against one," Charles said, grinning at the thought of the vacation he'd been pining for.

"Nova, seriously?" Ace groaned in annoyance. I smiled up at him, earning a quick kiss on the lips, and he sighed eventually giving in. "Well? Hawaii it is then," he sighed and Charles pumped his fist in the air repeatedly.

"Finally!" he yelled, pushing between me and Ace to sling his arms around both our shoulders. Ace looked a little annoyed at Charles and he shot him a look, which Charles promptly ignored.

"This is going to be great," Charles laughed, propelling us forward. I did my best to keep my balance as I stumbled, relying solely on Charles to hold me up.

"Not likely," Ace grumbled from beside him. I chuckled at the two boys who were the best of friends, but had nothing in common. Ace pulled away from Charles and grabbed my arm, leaving Charles all by himself.

"I'll meet up with you guys later so we can get going," Charles said, grinning as he walked away, off to who knows where.

"Are we actually going to Hawaii?" Ace asked, his huge black wings circling around me, and he rested his chin on top of my head.

"Yup," I smiled widely, hugging him back. We needed to

let loose and a live a little, and maybe a vacation was the way to do it, a break from everything stressful.

"You're crazy," he told me, kissing the top of my head.

"Crazy in love with you," I said and he just laughed, holding onto me like he never wanted to let go. I smiled inwardly, burying my face in his chest and breathed in deeply. I hadn't believed it before, when Ace had said it but now, after everything, I knew it had to be true.

Ace was my guardian angel.

# SIGMA'S BOOKSHELF

Sigma's Bookshelf (www.SigmasBookshelf.com) is an independent book publishing company that exclusively publishes the work of teenage authors, who are between the ages of 12 - 19. The company was founded in 2016 by Minnesota teenager Justin M. Anderson, whose first book, *Saving Stripes: A Kitty's Story*, was published when he was 14, and has since sold hundreds of copies.

"I know there are a lot of other teenagers out there who are good writers and deserve to have their work published, but don't have access to the kinds of resources I do. I wanted to help them," he said.

*Sigma's Bookshelf is a sponsored project of Springboard for the Arts, a nonprofit arts service organization. Contributions on behalf of Sigma's Bookshelf may be made payable to Springboard for the Arts and are tax deductible to the extent permitted by law. Donations can be made online at www.SigmasBookshelf.com/donate.*